DEAR SISTER DEAD

A LANIE PRICE MYSTERY

PERSIA WALKER

BLOOD VINTAGE
NEW YORK • MUNICH

Published by Blood Vintage Press

ISBN: 978-0-9816023-2-5

ABOUT THIS BOOK

Vera Kincaid had everything to live for. The wife of a wealthy preacher man, she was smart, beautiful, and popular. But lovely wives often have dark secrets. Vera was no exception. Society reporter Lanie Price investigates the death of a woman she held dear and finds out that, for Vera, forbidden love had deadly consequences.

To Cynthia Knudson

&

The Ladies of Highlands Ranch

CHAPTER 1

I t was eight o'clock at night. The early March weather was damp and chilly. I was shivering inside my coat and my feet were crying the blues. In getting dolled up for the evening, I'd been smart enough to grab my fur, but when it came to my feet, I'd chosen pretty over practical, picking T-strap shoes that were better suited for summer than late winter. Now, my feet were cold and wet and telling me to go home and get dry, to snuggle up in a blanket before my warm fireplace. But I hurried along, past my doorstep, determined to reach my goal.

The 139th Street block of Strivers' Row was for the most part empty and its windows dark, but the lights at number 128 were a different story. A soft light glowed behind the first-floor parlor window.

That particular townhouse belonged to the Kincaids, Vera and Levy. She was a retired nurse and he, the leader of one of Harlem's wealthiest and most influential churches. Both were highly respected, having worked long and hard for the benefit of the community. As it happened, they were also my neighbors. Lived only a couple of houses down from me. Normally, the thought of dropping by to see them brought nothing but pleasure.

I hurried up the steps of their limestone townhouse and knocked on their front door. Levy's face appeared in the wide parlor window. I waved. He frowned, let the curtain drop back into place, and disappeared. Seconds later, he opened the door.

The reverend was dressed in loose blue trousers and a gray silk smoking jacket with a velvet shawl collar. I recognized the jacket as the one Vera had given him for Christmas. I'd been with her when she picked it out. He held a leather-bound copy of the bible in one hand and rimless spectacles in the other. He wasn't a tall man, rather short actually, and had a bit of a paunch, but he was considered attractive. He had an olive-toned complexion and wore his salt-and-pepper hair in a conk, with smooth waves slicked back against his head. He sported a thin, well-manicured mustache and dressed well, spoke well. An educated man, dignified. A product of Tuskegee. He had charm. He had warmth. His parishioners loved him. Vera adored him. They'd been together for at least fifteen years.

He looked surprised and puzzled to see me and only me standing there. He glanced around and behind me. "Vera?"

"You mean, she's not here?"

"No," he shook his head. "Of course not. She—I thought —Weren't you two supposed to have—"

"She didn't show up."

He frowned. "What do you mean, she didn't—"

"She didn't. Show. Up."

He blinked, taking this in. His dark brown eyes again checked the empty space around me, as if he hoped she'd materialize out of thin air. When she didn't, his gaze returned to me. Only now, it held a glimmer of puzzled concern.

"Well, that's odd," he said.

I was cold and grumpy and now, whether I wanted to admit it or not, I was also getting a little worried. Where the heck was she if she wasn't here with him?

I stamped my feet to get the blood flowing. Two minutes of standing there and my toes had begun to feel like ice cubes.

"Levy," I said with just a hint of impatience. "May I come in?"

He made a startled little movement, murmured, "Of course," and stepped back, opening the door wide.

They had a perfect home, the Kincaids did. Levy's world was his church, Mount Olivet Congregational. He'd left the home decorating to Vera and had good results to show for it. She was Jamaican-born and the beauty of her heritage showed everywhere. It was a picture-perfect place of warm colors, amber lights, and lovely understated decorations. Vera's rose-scented perfume laced the air.

I followed him into the parlor. "She was supposed to have met me at Connie's Inn."

"Yes, that's what she told me. Dinner and a show afterward."

"She called me at the newsroom early this afternoon. I wasn't there, so they took a message. She said she might be a little late, but that I should go on ahead and hold the table."

"And?"

"And that's what I did. But she never came."

He shook his head. "That's really not like her. That's—"

The doorbell rang. He and I exchanged looks. Frowning, he went to the window and gazed out. His frown deepened. "It's some man. Some white man," he muttered. He placed the bible face down on the window seat and went to answer the front door.

A *white* man?

I could understand Levy's puzzlement—and irritation. What would a white man be doing in this part of Harlem at this time of night? Don't get me wrong. There was nothing special about seeing white folk in Harlem. But it was odd to see one in this part of it, especially at this time of day. Most of the time, they came uptown to binge or boogie in one of the clubs or speakeasies—not visit a resident in a quiet, respectable neighborhood late at night.

Of course ...

My heart skipped a beat.

There *was* one particular kind of white man who would be out at night, knocking on some poor man's door. The thought of him knocking on this man's door was enough to make my heart squeeze.

I hurried to the parlor entrance just in time to see Levy let the devil in.

CHAPTER 2

The devil. Okay, so maybe it was a little harsh to call him that. If you discounted the black beetle eyebrows, the ruddy complexion, and slightly pointed ears, then what you had left was a heart of gold. That said, it was rarely if ever good to have John Blackie appear on your doorstep.

He introduced himself to Levy, then glanced up to see me standing in the parlor doorway. His dark eyes narrowed and his lips tightened. He tilted his head as if to say, *How did you know?*

I didn't know but now I could guess. A little voice started to pray inside my head. *This is wrong. All wrong. It's gotta be.*

"Come on in, detective," Levy said. His voice was calm, too calm. Maybe, he didn't realize what a visit by Blackie usually meant. Maybe, he didn't realize that Blackie's day began when someone else's ended.

Blackie tipped his hat to me. Levy started to introduce us, but we both waved the introduction away, eyeing each other warily.

"That's OK," I said. "The detective and I, we know one another."

Blackie gave me a jaundiced eye. Whatever his mission, he was not happy to have me witness it. Levy started to lead Blackie into the parlor, but Blackie stopped him with a touch on the forearm.

"Reverend, can we speak privately?"

"Privately? What's this about?"

Blackie threw me another glance. *Go on. Leave.*

I pressed my lips together and shook my head. *Nope. No way. I'm not going nowhere.*

"Never mind," he said and gestured for Levy to lead the way. Once we were all in the parlor, Blackie said "Reverend, can you tell me the last time you saw your wife?"

"My wife? Vera? Why?" Levy threw me a look. The worry in his eyes was edging toward fear.

"Blackie, what's going on?" I asked.

"I think it would be better if I spoke to the reverend here alone for a minute."

"No," Levy said. "If this is about Vera, then I want Mrs. Price here to hear it. And it is about my wife, isn't it? That's why you're here. Something's happened to her."

Blackie hesitated, then said, "A woman's body has been found—"

Levy's eyes widened.

"Where?" I asked.

"Aground, near the ferry dock at Randall's Island. She was in the water before that. Washed ashore."

"Randall's Island?" Levy looked relieved. "Then you must be mistaken. That can't be Vera. She's never even been there. She'd never go there."

"Why do you say that?"

"Because," Levy shrugged. "She's my wife and I know her, and I know she'd never go there. She's afraid of the water, for one thing. Terrified of it. Why I can't even get her to take a stroll with me over on Riverside Park."

"The last time you saw her ... can you tell me what she was wearing?"

Levy thought for a moment. "She, uh, she was wearing a dark green suit, a brown coat and a hat. Oh, and that scarf you gave her, Lanie. I think it had flowers on it—?"

"Yes, lavender flowers and green leaves on an ivory background."

"Yes, she was wearing that, too," Levy said.

We both looked to Blackie.

"I'm sorry," he said. "Very sorry."

"Blackie, what makes you think it's her?" I asked.

"The papers she had on her. They were pretty clear." Blackie described the woman, what she was wearing, and the papers she carried.

Levy's relief evaporated. He backed away from Blackie, shaking his head and holding up his hands as if to ward off evil. "No, *no, no!* That can't be. That just can't be. Why I—"

He backed into the sofa and his knees gave out. He dropped down heavily, his eyes full of bewilderment. "I-I just spoke to her. Just a few hours ago. Before lunch. She was fine. That can't be her. This is a mistake, some kind of terrible mistake." He rubbed his temples. He sat there, like that, for several seconds. Then he looked to me. "Tell him, Lanie. You know my Vera. You know her. She-she can't be ... It just can't be her."

I looked from him to Blackie. "Was it a robbery?" I asked, then lowered my voice. "Or was it ... you know?"

"She still had her wedding ring and a pair of earrings. As for the rest, we, uh ... we don't know yet. But we don't think so." He addressed Levy. "I can say that we don't think she suffered. It was quick."

"How?" Levy asked. "How did she—"

Again, Blackie flickered his gaze at me. "You're not to print this, Lanie Price. D'you hear? You'll not print a word of this conversation."

"Of course not. But if it *is* Vera, then something will have to come out."

"There are certain details …." Blackie said.

"I understand, but first of all, I'm not here as a reporter. I came by as a friend—"

"To see the reverend?"

"To see Vera." I explained how she and I had had plans for the evening and she'd failed to show up. "I left the show after the first intermission and came here. I was too worried to pay attention, too distracted by the empty seat next to me, to just keep sitting there."

"You suspected trouble?"

"Well, I figured something had happened. But no, not this. I just knew that Vera's not the type to stand somebody up. Furthermore, she told me earlier today that she was coming but that she'd be late."

"Did she say why?"

"No." I told him about the message. "It didn't say much. Just that she had an errand."

"Nothing about what kind of errand?"

"Detective," Levy said. "You still haven't said what happened. Was there an accident?"

Blackie hesitated.

"Tell me," Levy said. "What happened to my wife?"

"She was shot," Blackie said, "in the back."

"Shot?" Levy's jaw went slack.

"We think she was running away from something —someone—"

8

"And the person shot her?" Levy said. "But who would do that? And why?"

Blackie made an open-handed gesture. "That, we don't know. Not yet." He sat on the edge of one of the fat armchairs positioned next to the fireplace. "Now, tell me again. When was the last time you saw her?"

Levy gazed at the black and white photograph of Vera that sat propped on the fireplace mantel. Next to it stood a wedding photo. Vera looked happy and Levy looked proud. There were no other photos. They'd never had children. Vera told me she'd had two miscarriages. The doctor told her she was risking her life every time she got pregnant. After that, they stopped trying.

"Levy would've made such a good father," she'd once told me. "Not having a child was a big disappointment to us and a big test of my faith. But I've come to terms with it. God's been kind to us, Lanie. And I'm grateful. I can't complain. I have a good man, and he has me. And really, he's all I need."

"It was around noon," Levy said, blinking back tears. "We were at the church office. I was working on my sermon for this coming Sunday. Vera stuck her head in, said she'd probably be away the rest of the day, that she was going to meet a friend for lunch and run a few errands. I knew she was going to meet Mrs. Price here for dinner and a show, so I was expecting her to come home late. I was sitting here, waiting up for her. I didn't know that anything was off—not till Mrs. Price here knocked on the door. She arrived just a few minutes before you did."

Blackie glanced at me and I nodded, affirming what Levy had said.

Blackie turned back to Levy. "Did she say who she was to meet or what the errands were?"

"I don't know. I don't remember." Levy frowned, trying

to concentrate. "Maybe she did. To tell you the truth, I was only half-listening. I was so caught up in writing my sermon for Sunday—so busy doing what I thought was the Lord's work—that I wasn't paying attention." He shook his head and with trembling hands covered his mouth. "God help me, I didn't do what I should've been doing. Honoring my wife. Listening to her. And now, you're telling me she's gone."

Blackie eyed Levy for several long moments. I knew that look. I could guess what he was thinking, that most female murder victims are killed by someone they know, and spouses, boyfriends, or lovers top the list. The ticking of the clock on the mantelpiece grew loud in the silence. Finally, Blackie spoke. His tone was neutral, the implication of his words anything but.

"My apologies, Reverend, but in cases like this, I have to ask. Where were you this afternoon?"

Levy blinked, then stared at Blackie. "Are you saying you think I did this? That I killed my wife?" His hands, resting on his knees, tightened into fists, his emotions switching from anguish to shock, and then anger.

"Nope," Blackie said. "I'm just asking you what you did this afternoon."

I don't know if Levy caught the edge in Blackie's undertone, but I sure did.

"Levy, it's just standard procedure," I said gently. "You don't have to answer, but the sooner you do, the sooner they can move on to looking at other people."

Levy clenched his jaw. You could see the muscles working under his skin.

"Reverend?" Blackie prodded.

To Blackie, the question was simple and routine. For him, Levy's resistance was puzzling, bewildering, likely even suspicious. But for Levy, the question was beyond insulting.

The suggestion that he would kill his wife, the women he loved—that he would commit such a heinous sin and so deeply violate his oath before his God in heaven and church on earth—was appalling.

"You dare … suggest that?" His voice was low and thick with not just grief but anger. "That I would kill my wife, the woman I loved above anything. That I would commit such a sin, so deeply violate my oath before his God. You suggest that I would do such a thing?"

"I suggest nothing, Reverend. Just asking a question."

A long minute passed. Then Levy took a deep breath and began to speak.

"I worked in my office all afternoon. My secretary, she'll vouch for me. She sits right outside my office door. I can't make a move without her knowing it." Here, he gave a weak smile. "Sometimes, I wonder. Who's in charge? She or me?" The smile went away. "Maybe she can even tell you who Vera was supposed to see. She knows Vera's schedule inside and out. She practically acted as Vera's social secretary. So, I recommend you check with her."

"Thank you," Blackie said. "Her name?"

"It's Denise. Denise Brown."

Blackie scribbled it down. "Can you think of anyone who would want to hurt your wife?"

"Do you really think it was someone who was after her, personally, and not just some random … hoodlum?"

"Like I said before, we don't know. I'm asking, just in case."

"Then I'd have to say, no." Levy shook his head numbly. "Everybody loved her. She was beautiful and kind and sweet. Everybody just loved to be around Vera."

Blackie and I exchanged glances. I'm sure we were

thinking the same thing, which was that if the killer was indeed a stranger, then that would make finding Vera's killer all the more difficult.

Blackie continued. "Can you tell me whether she acted strangely—perhaps, fearfully—in the last few days? Any sign that she was frightened or felt threatened or—"

"No," Levy shook his head. "Not at all. It must've been a stranger, 'cause no one we know would've done this kind of thing."

Again, Blackie and I exchanged looks. This time Levy caught us.

"You two really think that—"

"The police are just exploring possibilities," I said. "They have to do that. Check everything."

Levy sighed and nodded.

Blackie snapped his notepad shut, shoved it and the pencil into his side pocket, and stood up. "Reverend, I'm afraid I'm going to have to ask you to come downtown with me—to formally identify her."

Levy's face was a mask of ache. "Yes, of course."

We both stood.

"When can I have her back?" Levy asked.

"No more than a day or two."

Levy gave a slight nod. "Would you mind waiting here, detective, while I change?"

"Of course."

Levy moved like an old man. The news had aged him in an instant.

"So what about it?" Blackie said, turning to me. "Any idea who she was supposed to meet for lunch today?"

"You mean like somebody I didn't feel free to mention in front of the husband?"

He gave a small nod.

I shook my head. "Nope. I wouldn't know nothin' 'bout

that. But I can say that Vera wasn't the kind to be stepping out."

"You sure about that?"

"Why? You've heard something different?"

"No. It's just that ..." He drew a deep breath, let it out, and rubbed his forehead. "This one's going to be a tough one, Lanie. She was found in a place her husband says she would never go. And she was shot running away."

"Sounds like a kidnapping, actually."

"Maybe. It's as much a possibility right now as anything else."

"Did the bullet kill her or did she drown?"

"Most likely the bullet. It entered her back, just under her left shoulder blade. It cut right through her." He paused. "We noticed small bruises on her jaw and cheek. A couple of weeks old. You wouldn't know anything about that, would you?"

Again, I shook my head. "Fact is, I haven't actually seen Vera in oh, I'd say about a month. That was the point of tonight's get-together, to catch up with one another. We—"

"Ready," Levy said from the parlor doorway. He'd exchanged his smoking jacket for a business one, and put on his shoes and coat. He looked like a man who had it all: money, influence, respectability. But the grief in his eyes said otherwise. He did indeed have everything, except the one thing he cherished most.

Blackie and I preceded Levy out the front door. I watched Levy as he stepped out, then turned and carefully locked his door behind us. It brought back memories of how it was after my husband died. Such little rituals as locking up were sources of both comfort and pain: comfort because they represented the familiar in a world that had without warning turned upside down; pain because they were also a reminder of a shared life that had suddenly irrevocably come to an end.

We walked down the stairs together. Levy asked if he could drive his own car. Blackie said it would be better if they rode together. He'd make sure Levy got back home safely. I hugged Levy goodbye. He climbed into the police car. I walked a little ways away, then paused and watched as he was driven away.

CHAPTER 3

I first met Vera when my late husband, Hamp, joined Harlem Hospital as a doctor. Vera was one of the nursing supervisors. She and I became good friends. I loved her lilting, musical accent, her vivacious energy, and matter-of-fact but optimistic outlook on life. She was one of the most unsentimental people I've ever known, but loving, so loving, and warm and generous.

She was single when I met her. But soon afterward, she met a handsome young preacher. "He's different, Lanie. Different from the men I've known. I like him and I'm going to marry him."

"Does he know that? About the wedding plans, I mean?"

She'd smiled mischievously. "Not yet. But he soon will."

He was kind and down-to-earth, she said. "A good man, Lanie. A really good-hearted man. A man a woman can trust."

He was well-respected, she said, and the leader of a growing church.

It was as if they'd been made for one another.

Except for one thing.

"There's always a fly in the ointment, isn't there, Lanie? Nothing can be perfect. In our case, it's that he's Baptist and I'm Catholic, born and raised. My mother, if she were alive, would have a fit at the thought of me marrying someone outside the church."

"But you're going to do it?"

She thought about it. "I think I have to. He's everything I ever wanted, everything I've prayed for. And he wants me. So to say no to him, to send him away, it would be like spitting in the Face of God. Yes, this bit about religion is something I didn't count on. And there are other differences, changes, compromises I'll have to make. But it'll be worth it."

"You're sure?"

"As sure as a woman can be. This is a chance for me to grow. And it provides opportunities for me to make a difference. A real difference to women who need help."

He wasn't just a man of stature, she explained, but an effective advocate for social justice.

"When the white churches were shunting us aside, kicking us out, he stood up for the colored people in the community. Then he decided to go out and build his own church. He had to fight to do it, and I do mean fight. Had to go to court and battle those landowners in order to buy the property. Sometimes, he used their own tricks against them. And he won. He bested them. In their own courtrooms. He showed them what a colored man can do."

And he didn't stop there.

"Now he's building a community center, a place where young people can go and women can get help. Those are my interests, exactly. I can make a difference. With him at my side, I can change lives." She'd smiled dreamily. "In short, we're the perfect pair."

Now, that pair had been cleaved in two.

The day after they found her, Levy posted a substantial reward for information leading to her killer's capture. Meanwhile, Blackie gave a lean statement to the press that carried only the barest of details. He did take a few questions, however, not that his answers added all that much.

How long did she lay there before being discovered?

Not long. Maybe two hours.

Was it robbery or ...?

There was no evidence of either.

Well, what was the motive then? Who would want to kill a preacher's wife?

That, Blackie said wryly, *is the question of the day.*

I noticed that he didn't mention the bruises. "Did you do that on purpose?" I asked him later.

"That's one of the things I'm trusting you not to print."

"All righty."

After the news conference, I stopped by Levy's house to see how he was doing. The Kincaid's maid, Beulah Jean Henry, let me in.

"Oh, Miss Lanie," she said with a brave smile, her mournful eyes crinkling at the corners. "It's so good to see you. Come right in." She had worked for the Kincaids for the better part of ten years. Her eyes were red and her face slightly swollen. Her usually boisterous spirit appeared deflated.

"I'm so sorry this happened," I said.

"Thank you, ma'am." She closed the door softly and spoke in hushed tones. "Miss Vera was a good woman. Kind. Generous. Don't get no better than her."

"That she was. And the reverend, how's he doing?"

"About as good as can be expected. But that ain't all that good."

She offered to take my coat, but I told her I wouldn't be

staying long and followed her as she ushered me into the parlor. Levy was sitting in one of the armchairs by the fireplace, gazing into the flames, an open bible on his lap. I paused in the doorway.

Beulah took a step into the room. "Reverend?"

He didn't respond.

"Reverend, sir? It's Miss Lanie."

Still, he didn't move, didn't seem to have registered her voice or our presence.

"Levy?" I said, slightly raising my voice.

He gave a little jump and turned to see us. "Oh, I'm sorry. How long have you two been standing there? Beulah, show the lady in. Bring in some coffee."

Beulah gave me a little nod and faded away. I went in. Levy put the bible on the coffee table, then got to his feet. "I'm sorry, Lanie. I—Well, I guess I just floated off there for a minute."

"No apologies necessary. I—"

"People have been dropping by all day. They mean well, but ... It's a bit much."

"Oh, Levy, I didn't mean to—"

"Nah," he waved my apologies away. Come on in. Rest your feet."

We eased down in the armchairs. It was warm in the room, so I shrugged out of my fur. The thick coat slid off and fell in soft waves around me.

He sighed, rearranging the pillows behind his back. "I've been trying to get information about, you know, when I can have her back."

"What did they say?"

"Maybe in a day or two. They won't say for sure." He took his glasses off and let them dangle between his fingertips. "You know, me and her, we never did have that talk—that talk, you know? That every couple should have, about what we'd like in case … well, in case something happens. We always said we would, but we kept putting it off, putting it off. We thought we had all the time in the world. I mean, we *knew* we didn't. But we acted like we did. So much time. Now, time's run out. And I've been sitting here trying to figure out what she'd like." He looked at me, inviting my opinion.

"I'd say it would be something simple. Something elegant. A small circle of friends, of people who knew her, loved her."

He nodded, considering it. His gaze returned to the photographic portrait on the fireplace mantel. "People who knew and loved her. Hmph. Well, if we did it like that, the church would be overflowing. Cause there's a lot of people like that, you know, a lot of folks who loved her."

"Really?"

His gaze swiveled back to me. "Why? You don't think she was well-loved?"

"Oh, I know she was. I just don't believe she was all that well-known."

"I don't get you." He frowned.

"It's really quite simple. How many people actually, really knew her?"

"Oh, I see. Well, if you're going to be strict about it, I guess I'd have to say not many, or not all that many. My Vera was a very private person. She wasn't given to easy confidences or superficial friendships."

"Exactly."

"Yeah, but if I did it that way, the way you're suggesting and kept it small, then I'd have to deal with the matter of picking and choosing. Who's in the inner circle? Who's not?" He shook his head. "Funerals," he sighed, "are a lot like weddings. Lots of room for hurt feelings."

He put his glasses back on, shook his head. "So many

19

decisions to make, little ones and big ones and ... You know, over the years, I've counseled a good many people who've lost loved ones. I was always right there with the right words. I thought I was good at it. I thought I was saying the right things, that what I said was right and proper. Fitting. Now, I'm thinking back, recalling all those words, and I know they didn't mean a thing. There ain't nothing like this kind of hurt. Nothing like it."

What could I say? He was right.

He must've seen something in my face, because he gave a sad and slightly embarrassed half-smile. "What am I saying? Look who I'm talking to. You know what it's like. You've been there."

That I had. "Sometimes, losing Hamp feels like it happened yesterday. But there are other days, Levy, when it ... It's almost okay."

"Almost okay." He savored those words. For several seconds, he seemed to relax. But then the look of pained perplexity returned to his face. "The decisions, Lanie. The decisions. Like who to invite. The color of the casket. Whether it should be open or closed. That kind of thing. I know they're important. Supposed to be. But why? Why do they matter? Won't none of it bring her back."

I just let him talk.

He looked me an apology, with a sad smile and eyebrows drawn together. "Thank you for sitting here and listening to me ramble. I'm sure you've got better things to do."

"Well, I've got things to do. Sure enough. But they're not necessarily better."

That got a brief smile out of him. Then his expression turned serious again. "You know that cop, don't you, the one who brought the news?"

"Yes, he and I have crossed paths before."

"What do you think of him? Do you think he'll investigate, really investigate? Or will he just let it slide like a lot of them do?"

"No, he'll do his best. I'm sure of it."

"And will his best be good enough?"

"That I can't tell you, Levy. All I know is that he'll try. I've always known him to put his all into it."

"Well, I guess that's all I can ask for, isn't it? That the man tries."

"Has he been in touch?"

"No, I haven't heard a thing. Have you?"

I frowned, thinking it over. "Well, there's one thing he did ask me about. I'm not sure I should be mentioning it, but he'll probably be coming around to ask, anyway, so I might as well."

"Ask what?" The creases on his forehead deepened.

"About the bruises."

"What bruises?"

"Apparently, Vera had bruises on her face."

"Oh, those." He gave a dismissive wave. "She tried to hide them with makeup, but they kept coming through. Looked like dark smudges. I noticed them, asked her about them. She said she'd tripped and taken a tumble down the stairs." He gave a woeful smile. "She could be a bit awkward, you know. As graceful as a dancer, one minute. Clumsy as a giraffe, the next. Why, I've seen her trip on her own two feet while standing still."

"So, you took her explanation at face value?"

"About the bruises? Yes. Why?"

I took a moment to respond. "Well, the police…. They're wondering how she got them and whether…."

"Oh, I see." He nodded to himself. "I see. They're thinking that somebody gave her those bruises, hit her, and that the somebody who did that is the somebody who

killed her—and that that 'somebody'"—He made air quotes
—"is or might be *me*. Is that right?"

"It's one theory, yes."

"And what do you think, Lanie? What do you think,
knowing me?"

"I—"

"Because I would hope—no, I would *expect*—that you,
as a friend of the family, would know me better."

I shouldn't have risen to the bait. But I did.

"And I would've hoped that knowing me, knowing how
I felt about Vera, you would've known that I'd be asking
questions."

"And take my answers right back to that detective
friend of yours?"

"If it's the right answer, then my taking it to him, as you
put it, would only work in your favor. But the fact is, I
don't work for him. I work for the paper. I just want to get
the facts straight and I'd think you'd want me to."

He eyed me for a good long time, as if appraising me,
then dropped his gaze and let out long exhausted breath.
"I'm sorry. I know you're a friend. It's just that … This
whole thing. It's a nightmare. And I-I just can't wrap my
head around it. I can't believe that she's gone. And the way
it happened. That someone took her. Why would anyone
do that? Why?"

"Yes, that *is* the big question, isn't it? Why?"

Beulah entered, carrying a silver tray laden with tiny
porcelain cups, sugar cubes, thick cream, and a coffee pot.
She set it down on the coffee table and served us, then
started to go.

"Beulah, hold on a moment," Levy said.

She paused. "Yes, Reverend?"

"Would you know anything about those bruises Miss

Vera got on her face? How she got them? I wasn't here, if you'll remember. I was in Newark that day."

Beulah's eyes darted back and forth between Levy and me. Obviously, the question made her uneasy. She licked her lips and nodded. "Yes, I remember. That was two weeks ago last Tuesday. She tripped and fell down the stairs."

"Here, in the house?" I asked and took a sip of coffee. It was delicious, as usual.

"Yes'm. Right out there in the hallway." She gestured with a nod of her head.

"Did she go to the hospital?" I asked.

"No, ma'am. She said it weren't necessary, since she didn't break no bones or nothin."

Levy looked at me. "There. It's just as I said. I hope that satisfies you." He thanked her and she went her way.

When she was gone and the door closed behind her, I said, "It isn't a matter of satisfying me, Levy, but of satisfying the police."

"Well, you can tell them I wasn't here. And I've got the means to prove it."

"And what would that be?"

"All they got to do is call up the Hotel Madison. I stay there every time I have business in Newark. And that's where I stayed this time. Ask the manager. He knows me. He'll vouch for me."

"Well, I'm glad to hear it." I took one last sip, finishing the cup, then set it down and gathered up my coat and purse.

"You're going already?" He got to his feet.

"Yes, I'm sorry, but it's late."

"Of course."

"Let me know if there's anything I can do."

"Just keep an eye on that cop for me."

"Will do."

He thanked me and helped me with my coat. I gave him a quick hug and headed out.

Outside, standing on the sidewalk, I paused to wrap my scarf around my neck.

I hope that satisfies you, he'd said.

The problem was, it didn't. Nope, not at all. Not one bit.

And if I knew Blackie, it wouldn't satisfy him, either.

CHAPTER 4

I didn't sleep well that night and got up early the next morning. Of course, what was early for me was still late for everybody else. The newsroom was a beehive of activity when I got there. I swear, the only place louder was probably down on Wall Street. I went down there once, to the trading floor—don't ask why. It's a story for another day—and I never forgot the sound of the place. What with brokers yelling out puts and calls and whatnot, it was loud enough to make a woman go deaf.

Our newsroom wasn't as bad as that but it was close to it. Usually, by the time I got there, at around noon, the place was half empty, with folks out covering stories. But now, it was smack dab in the middle of the morning and the place was jumping.

Opening that door, I hit a wall of noise—the clacking of typewriter keys, the whooshing of the pneumatic tube, and the *thump-a-thump-thump* of the Associated Press wire service printer as it churned out reams of copy. Then there were the reporters chatting up sources on the phone, wheedling or needling, pleading or promising, using every tactic in the book to get them the information they needed.

I hung up my coat, placed my handbag in a desk drawer, then checked my stack of messages and mail. Nothing interesting.

Good. I didn't think I could handle 'interesting' that morning.

I headed to Sam's office. It was a bit of a glass bowl, giving him a view of the entire newsroom. Of course, that worked both ways. If he could see us, then we could see him, too. Our previous editor had kept his blinds down and his door shut. Sam kept the blinds down, too, but open. And his door was always more than ajar. He was reviewing a stack of copy when I knocked on his door. He waved me in. Usually, I'd leave the door open when talking to him but this time, I closed it.

"Take a seat," he said.

Sam already knew about Blackie's interest in the bruises. Now, I shared Levy's explanation.

"It doesn't make sense," Sam said.

"That's what I thought. A fall like that, down a flight of stairs, would've done more damage than just bruises to her jaw. At the very least, her arms and legs would've been black and blue."

"Do you think Levy hit her and forced Beulah to cover for him?"

"I don't want to think that, no. The question kept me up all night. I kept thinking back to Beulah, to that moment when he asked her about it, to see if … Oh, I don't know," I shrugged, "there was a look or something, anything like some kind of signal he gave her."

"And?"

"And nothing. There was nothing there. At least not so as I could see." I massaged my forehead. "The thing is, I just can't imagine him hurting Vera. I can't see him laying his hands on her, not like that. That man loved her. I mean, you should see him. He's like a shell, a ghost of himself."

"Hmph, well," Sam grunted. "Lanie, you know as well as I do that a man can beat the woman he loves just as easy as the one he don't. He can lay her low, put her down, then put on a big show, crying the blues."

"Even a man like Levy."

"Yup. Even one like him. Big? Important? Especially, a man like him?"

He wasn't wrong. I'd seen too many of those cases back in the day when I was covering the crime beat. Now that I covered society events, I didn't hear about home beatings or "home killings," as my mother used to call them, but I knew they happened among the rich as well as the poor.

The question was: Is that what happened to Vera?

Another day went by. There were no new developments. But late afternoon on the day after that, Levy called to say that the medical examiner had released Vera's body. He'd had the remains sent to the Duncan Brothers over on Lenox Avenue. The Duncans handled all of Harlem's elite. They'd done their work quickly, he said, and he was planning to hold a wake at the house the next day. Would I come? I said I'd be there.

BEULAH JEAN OPENED the door and gave me a warm if sad welcome. "Miss Lanie, it's always good to see you." She extended a hand toward the interior. "They're all in the parlor."

About twenty people were in there, chatting in muted voices. The church ladies in his congregation had made it their business to provide the reverend with food and flowers. I wasn't a member of Levy's congregation but because of my job I knew many of his congregants. They were busy, socially active women who belonged to any number of clubs, some just for the purpose of social climbing, but most because they believed in promoting social good. The husbands were there, too, not in as many numbers as the ladies, but enough to show their concern and respect.

"Where is she?" I asked Beulah.

"Come. I'll show you."

I followed her past the parlor to a room to the rear that the Kincaids used as a library. Its air of peace and quiet lent itself to the occasion. There were chairs for mourners to sit on and take their time. The casket, made of mahogany, stood in one corner. It was lined with cream-colored silk and generously bedecked with flowers. I was glad to see that Levy had opted to keep it open.

My lost friend. She looked beautiful, dressed in lace and ivory. The Duncan Brothers had done a wonderful job with her hair and makeup, a job reflective of their reputation. But even they, with all their skills and experience, hadn't been able to fully erase the effects of her last terrifying moments. Her face was still lovely, but it had aged. There was a sadness there I'd never seen before.

I bent closer and whispered both a prayer and a promise. "I'll find out what happened to you, dear sister. I promise. I'll find out, if it's the last thing I do."

I took one last long look, impressing her image into memory, knowing that this would be the last time I'd ever see her. Then I headed back to the parlor.

A TALL MAN leaned against the parlor's fireplace mantel, sipping coffee. Something about him was quite striking, something familiar, too. He stood apart from the gathering. I don't know if it was his youth, his clothing, his attitude, or all three. Most of the people there were comfortably in their thirties, forties, or fifties. A few were even in their sixties. He appeared to be in his early twenties. The rest of us were dressed in black, admittedly expensively, with attention to detail. He was in a cheap brown and gray suit, one that was faded and ill-fitting. As for attitude, his face bore an expression of contempt and resentment.

There was a slight pause in the conversation when I walked in. Then came nods of welcome, acknowledgment, and commiseration before conversation resumed. Levy saw me, raised his hand and started to break off the conversation he was having. But one of the other ladies jumped up and got to me first. It was Mrs. Dill, Mrs. Coriander Dill. Short, stout, and sleek, she was one of the most powerful women in Harlem society. Her presence was a testament to Vera's high standing in the community and to how much she meant to us.

"How are you, Mrs. Dill?"

"Not well. None of us are. Not really. Our dear Vera. Not only gone—but murdered! Can you imagine?"

"I—"

"I heard you were here when the cops brought the news." She threw a conspiratorial glance over her shoulder, leaned forward, and whispered. "Do they suspect the reverend?"

"Why would you think that?"

"Because they always do, don't they? When they can't figure out who did it, they blame the spouse. I just hope they don't try to make him a scapegoat. It would be such a travesty of justice. Unthinkable."

"Well, I—"

"You'll make sure the cops investigate, really investigate, won't you? You and that paper of yours, you'll hold their feet to the fire?"

"We'll write the story, yes. Whether we'll—"

"Good. That's all I wanted to hear. We were waiting for you to show up."

We?

She glanced over to a little cluster of women sitting together, all sipping from dainty cups, pinkies raised, and observing us. I gave them a slow nod and they gave me one in return, all together, as though they were all of the same mind, which, of course, they more or less were.

"Mrs. Dill, I really—"

She grabbed me by the hand. "Here, there's someone I think you ought to meet."

With that, she pulled me across the room. To my surprise, I found myself standing in front of the odd young man. Mrs. Dill began the introductions.

"Mrs. Price, this is Vera's younger brother, Mr. Martin Del Ray—"

"Oh," I murmured, extending a hand.

Now, I understood why he seemed so familiar. Up close, the resemblance was clear. However, Vera had never mentioned to me that she had a brother, or any siblings at all, for that matter, so I was surprised to see that she had one.

"Mr. Del Ray," Mrs. Dill continued, "this is Mrs. Lanie Price. She's a society columnist." Mrs. Dill beamed. "A lady of great reputation. She'll make sure we find out the truth about what happened to our dear Vera and that her story is written up properly."

He straightened up and shook my hand. It was a firm shake, crisp.

"It's good to meet you," I said. "I'm just so sorry it's under these circumstances. "

"You knew my sister well?" He sounded like Vera, too. Had her accent. Even in those few words it revealed itself.

"I thought of her as one of my dearest friends."

"Oh! Excuse me," Mrs. Dill said, clasping her hands together. "But there's someone who's just arrived, I have to go and see. I'll be right back," she said and hurried off.

Martin Del Ray shook his head. "She's quite a character."

"I guess you could say we all are. But you don't like us very much, do you?"

"Us?"

"The people here." I twirled my finger to indicate everyone in the room, and then lightly tapped myself on the shoulder, "including me."

He looked slightly guilty. "Whatever gave you that idea?"

I noticed he hadn't denied it. Instead, he'd answered a question with a question. "Your stance, the look in your eyes as you observe the room."

He inclined his head. "My, aren't you observant?"

"I try to be. It's how I earn my bread and butter."

"Vera used to tell me she had a friend who was very smart, very direct, and who wrote for the papers. I take it that's you."

"You have the advantage. I'm afraid she never mentioned you to me."

He shrugged. "That doesn't surprise me."

"Wh—?" I said, starting to ask him why, but Mrs. Dill's shrill voice and the sound of a tapping spoon interrupted.

"Excuse me! Excuse me, everyone!"

31

I turned to see Coriander Dill, standing at Levy's side, tapping a teacup with the edge of a a spoon to get everyone's attention.

"The reverend has a few words to say to us," Mrs. Dill said.

The murmur of conversation subsided. People sat upright to listen, balancing their tea cups on their laps.

Levy thanked Mrs. Dill, then began."My wife," he said, "my dear, dear Vera …"

To be honest, I didn't hear the words that followed. I'm not sure I registered them at all. His pain was palpable. A wave of ache washed over me, left me reeling with the realization of having lost her, of what we'd all lost.

I've never considered myself the best of friends. I don't stay in contact the way I should. I fail to offer invitations when I should. And I don't always respond to offers when I should. And so I'd put off seeing her for far too long. I'd assumed that we'd have time. I'd taken it—taken *her*—for granted.

As I stood there, watching Levy, I recalled the pain of losing Hamp. That kind of pain abates but never entirely goes away. It's always there, a monster in the closet, waiting to jump out, claws ready. And it chooses when and where it'll emerge. Sometimes … Well, sometimes, you think you can prepare for it, steel yourself against it, but you're always wrong. It always manages to ambush you, to take you unawares and ill-prepared.

Levy finished with a call to prayer. "Everyone please join here in a circle and hold hands."

I started forward, then noticed that Martin Del Ray held back. "You're not going to join in?"

"I don't believe in a god who lets white folk do what they do. And if I did, I wouldn't believe that the reverend over there is in any way fit to be leading me to Him."

Talk about being direct, I thought. *I guess I'm not the only one.*

I left him. The prayer circle didn't take long, no more than fifteen minutes, with everyone adding their own words of praise to Vera's memory and prayer for the sanctity of her soul. Afterward, more than a few people wanted to talk to me, either about Vera's case, or the last criminal case I'd written about, the double murder of a Cotton Club dancer and a well-loved photographer. It took me half an hour to get back to Martin Del Ray, but I finally did. I'd been aware of his resentful gaze on our host the whole time.

Back at his side, I lowered my voice. "I take it you don't like Levy."

"Like him? I can't stand him—him and everything he stands for."

"Oh, and what, in your opinion, is that?"

He grimaced. "He likes to play Mr. Big-shot. But he's just another Negro kowtowing to Mr. Man."

"You do know his history, don't you? He started out with nothing. He's has to fight for every inch he's ever gotten."

"So, you're an apologist for his kind. I should've known better."

"Apologist? I've got nothing and no one to apologize for. I simply want to make sure you know who you're talking about."

"Know him? Yes, I know him. Vera used to preach to me about what a fine man he is. Same kind of stuff you're telling me. About how he fought to get the church land."

"But you don't believe it?"

"What I *believe* is that all you dicties, all you're trying to do, is copy the white man. You're not interested in Mother

Africa. You're not interested in learning about our roots, our history. You're—"

"Oh, I see," I said, recognizing his rhetoric. "You're a Garveyite, aren't you? A follower of Marcus Garvey's Back-to-Africa movement?"

"No. A Communist." He eyed me, apparently expecting to see me clutch my pearls in dismay. When I didn't, he said, "That doesn't throw you off?"

"Should it?"

"It's just that, I would've thought that since you're ..."

"What? One of *them*? A *dicty*? A member of the *bourgeoisie*?"

"Well, now that you mention it, yes."

In fact, the news that he was a communist had indeed thrown me off but not for the reason he supposed. Vera was a traditionalist when it came to politics. Yes, she was socially active, but she believed in working inside the system. She was skeptical, even distrustful, of any beliefs outside the mainstream. If her brother held 'radical' views, then it might've driven a wedge between them. It would help explain why she had never mentioned him to me.

"So, you two weren't close?"

"Is that any of your business?"

"Were you?"

He paused. "We tried."

"What does that mean?"

"It means ... that we weren't as close as I would've liked. My fault, I guess. I made her uneasy."

I could well believe that. "You saw her often?"

He shook his head. "I've been away a long time, in Moscow. Studying with Lovett Fort-Whiteman. You've heard of him?"

I had, indeed. "He's a firebrand. Brilliant in many ways.

An idealist. But more than a little bit ahead of his time. And more than a bit naive."

He was slightly bitter. "You would say that. You sound like my sister."

"Yes, well, I take that as a compliment. She was very wary of fake prophets. 'Fake Moses,' she used to call them."

He grunted. "She was a fine one to talk, given the man she was married to."

It was time to bring the conversation back to him. "When did you get back?"

"Three weeks ago."

"Got a job."

"Why? You going to offer me one?"

"No, just being curious."

"Well, I'm working for the Party. We've got offices over on West 124th Street." He paused, eyeing me. "You should stop by sometime."

It was a challenge. It was a thought. "Maybe, I will."

He laughed.

"You don't believe me," I said.

He inclined his head. "Like I said, you're—"

"One of them. Yes, I know. But, well, you never know."

He glanced around, then leaned in close and lowered his voice. "Look, I know you can't say too much, being a reporter and all, but tell me, what really happened to my sister? And what are the police doing about it? Levy won't tell me a thing."

"That's probably because he doesn't know anything to tell. As far as I know, the police don't know what she was doing there—"

"By the river?"

"Yes." I paused, hoping he would have something to add, but he didn't, so I went on. "It's not even clear if that's where she entered the water."

"So, she could've gone in somewhere else and floated ..."

"Exactly," I said. "Have the police spoken to you?"

He shook his head. "I'm not sure they even know I exist —at least, not with regard to this."

I wondered what he meant by that, and was about to ask when he went on.

"I guess I should go see them."

"Will you?"

"I don't know yet. Perhaps. But we both know that the cops are not our friends. Interactions with them, they often don't end well for us."

Though he was speaking in general terms, I had the distinct impression that his rancor was born of personal experience.

"If you did go, what would you tell them?"

His gaze went to his sister's framed photo on the mantel. He picked it up, studied it. "That's a good question. I'm not sure. It depends on what they want to know."

"Well, if you've been away a long time, they might not think you have anything worthwhile to add. For example, they've been asking whether Vera had enemies, anyone out to harm her. Whether she'd been acting fearful or worried. They might not think you have anything to say about that ... since you were away for so long." I drew out the last few words in an unspoken question.

He set the picture back down. "Just because I was away, it doesn't mean we were out of touch. We exchanged letters every few months."

"And did she ever mention—"

"Enemies? No. She never said anything ... about that."

There was a slight hesitation, a slight change in his tone of voice.

"About that?" I repeated. "But she did say something—about something else?"

He took a moment, obviously trying to determine whether he could trust me. "She wasn't happy."

"No?"

"No."

"Why not?"

"She wasn't being true to herself. She couldn't be, not when married to a man like him." He nodded toward Levy.

I wasn't sure what he meant by that. Vera had told me the very opposite, that her marriage to Levy would enable her to be more of herself, to develop and grow and accomplish what she'd set out to do, help young mothers, recruit and train better nurses—all of which she'd done, using her influence as the wife of a powerful preacher.

He gestured toward Levy. "She gave up too much for him, too much of the woman she was, the woman she could've been. And whether she was willing to admit it or not, she regretted it."

"She told you that??"

He paused, then said, "She didn't have to."

"Then how—"

"I know because she was having an affair. No one does that when they're happy or satisfied."

"An *affair?*" For a moment, I stood there, open-mouthed, shocked. "But you're wrong. You've got to be. Vera would never—"

"I saw her. With him, the man."

"Saw her? You just saw her with a man and you assumed—"

"They were sitting together, in the back of a restaurant talking, in the corner, their heads close."

"How close?"

He drew his palms together. "Very close. They were in a

world of their own. Whatever they were saying, it was for them and them alone."

I had a rather sudden and very earnest desire for a good strong drink. "When was this?"

"About a week ago."

I was about to ask about the man, for a description, when I heard my name being called—"Lanie?"— and turned to see Levy approaching.

"This character hasn't been bothering you, has he?" Levy asked.

"I've been filling her ears with all sorts of nonsense," Del Ray said. "And she's been gracious enough to listen. But," and here he set his coffee cup on the fireplace mantel, "I think it's time for me to head out."

"Oh, must you?" Levy asked with no attempt at sincerity.

Del Ray pointedly ignored him and said to me, "It was nice meeting you. It truly was."

"Same here," I said.

The two men gave each other the evil eye. Then Martin Del Ray took his leave and Levy watched him go. He kept tabs on him as he made his way through the crowded parlor, watched him as if he thought his young brother-in-law might pocket some of the silverware along the way.

"You don't like him," I said.

"I don't trust him. He's a blowhard. Talks big, does nothing. He was always a nuisance. Gave Vera a ton of headaches. Then he was away for a while—thank goodness —but now he's back, being a pest. He made Vera miserable."

I started to ask for specifics, but Levy held a hand up. "I don't want to bother you with petty family politics. We're here to honor Vera's memory. Let's do that."

I said brightly, "Of course. The service is tomorrow?"

"I've been working all day on the right words to say. I don't think I've got them. My own wife and I don't know what to say." Ss

"Speak from the heart, Levy. Just speak from the heart."

I stayed for a while longer, talking to Levy and the others. But my thoughts were on Martin Del Ray and the timing of his return.

CHAPTER 5

"Vera's brother sounds like a character," Sam said the next morning.

"That he is."

'You think he might've done it?"

"I don't know. He's got a temper. And he certainly seemed to feel that she had somehow betrayed 'what she stood for,' whatever that was."

Sam paused. "You know that name, Martin Del Ray, it sounds familiar."

"You think you've heard it in connection to something?"

He considered it, then shook his head. "I don't know."

"By the way," I said, "I was able to get the manager of the Madison Hotel on the line this morning."

"And?"

"He checked the register and found Levy's name there."

"So, the reverend was indeed in Newark the day his wife got those bruises. Relieved?"

"Yes ... and no." I drummed my fingers against the dark wood of the armrest slowly, thoughtfully.

"What does that mean?"

"It means that there are two stories here: the one the housekeeper told and the one the bruises tell. They still don't reconcile."

He considered that. "The thing is, bruises don't lie."

"No ... no, they don't, do they?" I said with a sigh. *Bruises don't lie.*

DESPITE THE CHILLY MARCH DAY, the doors to Levy's church stood open. Ushers in black suits and white gloves were positioned on either side of the entrance. I won't say I arrived early, but I sure didn't arrive late. Nevertheless, the place was packed by the time I got there. People were sitting shoulder to shoulder, with young children balanced on their knees. The air was thick and humid and close, a slightly suffocating mixture of perfume and cologne, spiced with sweat.

The ceremony was what one would've expected. Solemn. Refined. Marked by both grief and a certain determined dignity. A sea of black veils hid swollen eyes. Every now and then, there was the flutter of a white lace handkerchief as it was used to delicately dab away tears.

Vera's touch had blessed so many of these lives. Whether it was by mentoring the young nurses who worked under her at Harlem Hospital, tutoring children after hours to advance literacy, or counseling young mothers on nutrition, Vera had not only helped a great many of these people, but also given them the tools to help themselves. That was her lasting legacy.

I recognized many of the faces. There was Coriander Dill and her husband, Ian; Mamie King and her daughter-in-law, Tessie; Dr. Joplin and his two daughters; and my lawyer neighbor, David McKay.

Beulah Jean Henry. She was there, too. The housekeeper caught me looking her way. She inclined her head and her lips bowed in a soft, sad smile.

The one face I most definitely did not see was that of Vera's brother. I can't say I was surprised.

Levy's voice rang out strong and true. His words were a balm to the grieving heart. He was a talented orator and he did not disappoint. Even so, at times, I found my attention wandering. I scanned the crowd around me, noting the men, in particular. Martin Del Ray might not have been there, but his words were ever present in my mind.

She was having an affair.

I found that so hard to believe. But if it were true, then was the man here, among the mourners? I went from face to face, dismissing one after the other. *Too young. Too old. Too immature. Too pretty. And that one? Too damn married.* I shook my head at myself when I caught myself thinking that one.

After the ceremony, I joined the line of mourners to briefly hold Levy's hand and murmur more words of condolence. He thanked me and after a brief exchange, I moved on.

I went down the steps and paused. It must've rained while we were inside, because the streets were damp. However, the sun had come out and it alleviated some of the gloom. It did not, however, warm the day's chill. I turned up my collar and wrapped my coat tightly around me, shivering.

I didn't have to wait long.

Beulah Jean appeared not five minutes later. She left by a side entrance. I walked in her direction. "Beulah! Beulah Jean!"

Surprise lit her face. "Oh, hello, Miss Lanie! Will you be stopping by the house later?"

"Another day, no doubt, but no, not today." I interlaced my arm with hers and we started walking back toward Strivers' Row, which was only a few blocks away. "I did want to speak with you again, though. So, I'm glad to find you here."

"Me, Miss Lanie? You want to speak with me? Why? Is there something wrong? I mean—?"

"Well, perhaps. I do think there's more to the story of Miss Vera's bruises than you've told me."

She came to a stop and put her hand to her chest. "Miss Lanie, I don't lie. I—"

"No, maybe not. But you do—or in this case, did—omit some important details, didn't you?"

Her gaze edged away.

"Come o. Let's keep walking," I said.

A look of fear shot across her face. She swallowed and tears welled in her eyes. She paused to snap open her clutch and grab a plain handkerchief. "I'm so sorry," she sniffled.

"That's all right. Just tell me the rest of what happened."

She dabbed at her eyes, then folded up the handkerchief and stared down at it. "What do you want to know?"

"Was Miss Vera alone when she had her accident?"

She was quiet for a moment, working the handkerchief. Then she shook her head. "No."

"Who was with her?" I steeled myself inwardly to hear her say Levy's name.

She swallowed. "It was Mr. Martin."

"Mr. Martin?" I whispered. "Miss Vera's *brother?*"

"Yes, ma'am. He was with her."

Martin. Martin Del Ray. It took me a moment to adjust to *that* news. "Did he hit her?"

"No. He, uh ... well, he pushed her. I mean, she pushed him and—"

"Slow down. Just take it one step at a time."

"Okay." She rubbed her forehead. "What happened was this: they was arguing. Ever since he came back, they'd get to arguing. But this time, it ... it got bad. He told her that she'd betrayed her people and that one day she was gonna regret it."

"Were those his exact words?"

"Pretty much, ma'am. That's what he said."

"Okay. Go on."

"And he accused her of—I don't even wanna say it, ma'am. I surely don't. I don't believe in saying bad things about the dead when they ain't here no more to defend themselves."

"I understand. But you yourself, you're not saying anything about her. You're simply telling me what he said."

"But—"

"I know. You want to defend her reputation. That's what we all want. But we can't do that if we don't know what to defend it against." I paused to let that sink in, then said, "And you know what else is important?"

She looked at me with an expression of defeat. "No, ma'am."

"It's just as important to find her killer, to figure out who hurt her."

Her shoulders slumped. "All right. Yes, ma'am. I understand. I just," she sighed. "I just didn't want to get caught up in nothing."

"Are you afraid of Mr. Martin? Is that why you said she fell down the stairs and didn't mention that he was there?"

"Afraid of Mr. Martin? No. Not at all."

"Then why—"

"She told me to say that. She said that if anybody asked,

That's what I was to say. And that I was to keep Mr. Martin's name out of it."

Hmph. I considered that for a moment. "Do you think he could've hurt her like that?"

"Who? Mr. Martin?"

I nodded.

Her eyes widened and she put a hand to her heart. "You mean ... killed her?" she whispered.

Again, I nodded.

The worried frown creasing her forehead deepened. Slowly, she shook her head. "I wanna say no, ma'am. But in all honesty, I just don't know. He don't strike me as no violent man. But he's ..." She paused.

"Yes?" I prodded when she didn't speak further. "He's what?"

"Well, I guess you could say he's passionate, you know? He believes what he believes and he don't brook no disagreement. Now, Miss Vera, she could be pretty stubborn and set in her ways too, you know. But she didn't hold a candle to the stubborn, dig-your-heel-in-the-ground, don't-give-up-no matter-what kind of stubbornness, I done seen in Mr. Martin."

We stopped at the corner for the light.

"You know Mr. Martin and the reverend, they don't get along," she said. "I guess you saw that at the wake."

"I sure did."

"Well, the funny thing is, in some ways they ain't all that different. I mean, they both loved her, but they ... well, the way they showed it was by trying to control her. I guess they thought they was trying to protect her. But that meant they ended up treating her like a child, like she didn't know who she was, like they thought they knew her better than she knew herself."

The light changed and we started walking again.

"I dunno." She gave a little shrug. "You shouldn't be listening to me. I'm just shooting off at the mouth and I shouldn't be. I mean, what do I know? I don't know nothing."

"I think you do," I said. "I think you know a lot. And I appreciate your honesty."

We had reached the corner of 139th and Strivers' Row.

"If you remember anything more," I said, "please feel free to tell me. I promise I'll be real careful with whatever you say."

"All right, ma'am. Thank you."

I watched her walk down the block, a small figure in a humble hat and coat. When she reached the Kincaid residence, she paused and looked up at it. She stood there for several seconds, as if working up the courage to go back in. Finally, she drew a deep breath, climbed the stairs, unlocked the door, and went inside.

CHAPTER 6

B ack at the newsroom, Sam was on the phone, leaning back in his office chair. I rapped on his door, went in, and took a seat. He ended his call, so I started to speak, but he raised an index finger.

"I have news for you," he said. "Remember how I told you that Vera's brother's name sounded familiar? Now, I know why." He pulled a folder from the pile stacked at his elbow. "Martin Del Ray told you he just got back in town, right? Well, he was telling the truth there. But what he didn't tell you is that he was in jail before that."

"What for?"

"Exercising his First Amendment rights." Engaging in freedom of speech. Always a dangerous thing for a colored man to do.

"A couple of years ago, he was in St. Louis, talking to a dozen or so party members. He pushed for ending housing segregation, better protections for tenant workers, and U.S. formal recognition of the Soviet Union. Unfortunately for him, there was a spy in the audience. One of J. Edgar's men. He reported that Del Ray openly advocated 'resistance to the United States.' It was a lie, of course. An exaggeration. But ..."

"It was just what Hoover wanted to hear."

"Exactly."

"Well, everybody knows Hoover's got a thing for any colored man interested in civil rights and labor. He's sure the main reason the Communist Party wants to recruit us colored is to get us to help them overthrow the government."

"You said it. The Bureau already saw Del Ray as dangerous. That speech he gave made them see red. They arrested everybody there, but he was the only one they charged. Accused him of sedition. Of course, Del Ray protested. Said he'd done nothing treasonous."

"But he probably got carried away by the moment and used a phrase for two he shouldn't have—basically made Hoover's job easy for him."

"Probably," Sam said. "The charges were ultimately dropped, but not before he'd been behind bars for a while."

"What's 'a while?'"

"Less than a year. But long enough. It's not just the time; it's what they do to you while you're serving it."

"No wonder he went off to Russia," I said. "After being jailed like that, he probably couldn't wait to leave."

"You said he was over there studying with Lovett Fort-Whiteman?"

"Yup."

"Well, Fort-Whiteman came back from Moscow not too long ago, too. His main job now is to recruit American colored to join the American Negro Labor Congress. And Del Ray is probably helping him." He tossed me the folder.

I opened it to find several clips of newspaper articles,

all of them on Del Ray. "A 'communist.' A 'radical,'" I read out loud. "Vera probably wasn't happy with that."

"Most middle-class colored people aren't. And for the same reasons DuBois doesn't hold with Garvey."

"They think radicalism makes us looks bad, that Hoover and his ilk can use it against us."

"What do you think?" Sam asked.

I looked up from the news clippings. "I don't know. Lovett Fort-Whiteman, Marcus Garvey. I agree with their ultimate goals—equality, independence, opportunity, freedom from the fear of the noose. I think most of us do. It's their methods that worry me. I sure don't hold with Booker T. I guess I'm closer to DuBois than any of them. And you?"

"The same."

I looked back down at the articles. "I can see where Vera's brother's radicalism would've caused problems between them."

"Read further. It wasn't just Del Ray who was involved. Vera was once involved, too."

My jaw dropped. "That's not possible."

Sam pointed to the file. "Keep reading."

I flipped through the articles, scanning them quickly. Sure enough, more than one mentioned Vera. "According to these, the police thought she was a fairly high-ranking member of one of these suspect groups. But that's so hard to believe." I closed the folder. "That doesn't sound like her, not at all. That's just not the Vera I knew."

"Well, maybe—"

"Don't say it. Just don't."

"I won't. I don't have to. You can see it for yourself."

You didn't know her. I'd stopped Sam from saying it, but at that moment, I couldn't stop myself from thinking it.

Maybe you didn't know her, not nearly as well as you thought you did.

"There's more," I said. "Isn't there? I can tell from the look on your face that there's more."

He raised an eyebrow and pointed to the folder again. "The reports in there say that when Del Ray was arrested, the feds here in New York went and questioned Vera."

"And?"

"And it was right after *that*, right after talking to her, that they filed charges against him."

I drew back. "No."

"Yes."

"You're saying that Vera betrayed her own brother?"

"I'm saying that's what it looks like."

I thought about it, shook my head, still resisting, refusing to believe—

"Sam, we both know that the police are real good at setting people up, making it look like they collaborated when they didn't."

"They sure are. So, maybe she did; maybe she didn't. The point is that it was made to look as though she did."

I sighed a small sigh of relief, grateful that he'd at least conceded that point. "Did he or anyone in the Party make threats against her?"

"Some did, right when it happened. People were pretty convinced that she'd talked. And more than one person said she needed to pay for it."

I reopened the file, reviewed the paperwork again. "If ... if it's true that she was with this group, and I'm still not sure it is, then it looks like she broke with it right around the time she married Levy. So maybe Levy pressured her—"

"Or maybe she saw a chance at a nice life and decided that betrayal was worth it."

"No. That can't be, Sam. Vera wouldn't have done that."

"Look at the timeline. It speaks for itself."

"Maybe." I closed the folder. "But maybe not. There's a lot going on here that we still don't understand. I'm not going to believe Vera betrayed anybody until a lot more comes to light."

Sam raised his hands. "Hey, I'm not your enemy. And I'm not accusing her. What I'm saying is that looks count. That could be enough for some people."

I worried my lower lip. Sam was right. It didn't matter whether she'd actually betrayed anyone. It just mattered that someone might've thought she had.

The thought that Del Ray or one of his people might've killed his own sister filled me with an enormous sadness. I'd liked him, liked his passion and his fire, his sense of rebelliousness. And he'd given me the feeling that he truly loved her. But people have been known to kill the ones they love. That he could've had a hand in her death, intentionally or otherwise, made a disheartening kind of sense.

"The question is, why would he have done it, now?" I mused.

Sam shrugged. "Maybe he didn't have time to do it before. He was in such a hurry to leave the country that ..." Sam paused, and inclined his head. "And maybe, he didn't even intend to kill her. They met, had an argument, tempers got heated, and ..." His voice trailed away.

I nodded, thinking about it. "It's ... not impossible," I said reluctantly and told Sam what Beulah had said.

"So, it was Del Ray who gave her those bruises," Sam said. "It shows he's got a temper. It—" He straightened up and his gaze shot past my shoulder to the newsroom. "Speak of the devil ..."

"What?"

51

He gave a nod and I twisted around to see Martin Del Ray in the flesh. He was sitting in the visitor's seat at my desk and one of my fellow reporters was hurrying down the aisle to Sam's office, beckoning me.

CHAPTER 7

Vera's brother was not the cool cucumber I'd seen at the wake. His shoulders were hunched and he was jogging his right knee, tapping it.

"They're after me," he said by way of opening.

"Who's after you?" I sat down, laying the closed file on my desk.

"The cops. They think I did it. Yesterday, they came to see me. Some Irish detective. He said my sister had bruises. Asked me if I knew where she got them. I told him what happened. But I don't think he believed me. I think he's coming back, to arrest me."

I leaned forward. "What exactly did you say?"

"I told him the truth. Just as I'm telling you."

"And that was?"

"That we fought. We argued about the choices she'd made. And then I told her I'd seen her with that man. I told her that even though I can't stand Levy, I didn't think she should be cheating on him. That it wasn't right. Our parents would be ashamed of her. She told me to mind my own business. Got angry. Told me to leave. And then she shoved me and I shoved her back and she tripped and fell."

"Down the stairs?"

"The *stairs*? No, we were in the parlor. She hit her face on the coffee table."

His story made sense. It explained the pattern of bruises. "And that's it?"

"That's it."

I glanced at the folder, thinking of its contents. "You said you argued with her about choices she'd made."

"Yes."

"So, there were hard feelings there."

"No-yes."

"Which is it?"

"Both. But ..."

"But what? One of those 'choices' was to leave the Party. That must've made you angry."

"No, I—"

"Then you were arrested and she snitched on you—"

"No, she—"

"Abandoned you."

"*No!*"

"Betrayed you—"

"*NO!*" He slammed my desk with the palm of his hand so hard that others in the newsroom turned to look. I raised a hand to signal that everything was under control.

He leaned toward me, lowered his voice, and spoke through clenched teeth. "She didn't do that. She didn't do any of that. Look, we disagreed on a lot of things, but she was my sister, my *big* sister, and her whole thing was about taking care of me."

"But that would've made it hurt even more, wouldn't it? That the big sister who'd always protected you turned her back on you and hung you out to dry?"

He sat back, exhausted, with an expression that clearly said, *What's the point?* Then he pushed his chair back and stood. "You sound like that detective. Maybe it was a mistake to come here."

I gazed up at him. "Why exactly did you come?"

"Because I want the truth to come out. Because if I'm arrested and something happens—and you and I both know that things do happen to colored men in police custody—then I want to make sure the press gets it straight. I make to make sure that you people, and the people who read you, know that I didn't have nothing to do with my sister's death. I don't want them making me the patsy, sweeping her death under the rug, and letting the real killer go free. Is that answer enough for you?"

If he was lying, he was good at it. I sat back in my chair. "I'm listening."

He hesitated, glanced around at the still curious faces watching us, watching *him,* then dropped back down in the seat. He ran a hand over his closely cropped hair, then leaned on my desk and gazed intently into my eyes.

"Look, Vera didn't snitch on me. She didn't do that. Not exactly. But yes, of course, when it happened, when she talked to the feds and said what she said, it hurt like hell. But *kill* her over it? Shoot her and leave her in the river like that? Never. She was all I had. She raised me from the time I was little, from when our parents died. I looked up to her. She's the one I always turned to. Yeah, it hurt to see her lose her way like that, but I loved her. And respected her. I never would've hurt her."

I considered what he'd said, considered him. "Fine," I said, thinking of the contents of the folder. "But what about someone else? Could someone in the Party have wanted her to punish her?"

He moved his jaw. "I don't want to think that. But I don't know."

"Maybe you should think about it."

"All right, then. I'd have to say that wouldn't make sense."

"Why not?"

"First, why wait so long? Second, she was never a member."

"I have information that she was."

His eyes narrowed. Intuitively, they shot to the folder. "Oh," he said. "I see. You've been reading up on me."

"Well?"

He shook his head. "No, she was never a part of it. Not really. Did she display some interest? Yes," he nodded. "She was educated and she was smart, and she cared—really cared—about helping people. But she never got into the Party. Not real deep. Not like me. She believed in the goals, but she didn't believe in the politics, the theory. She used to give me money when she had some, help me out here and there. And she helped me write up some pamphlets, edited this little newsletter I had going. But that was as far as it went."

"This help she gave you, it continued even after she married Levy?"

"Yeah, even then. Of course, he didn't know anything about it. I'm sure she didn't tell him. Then everything went south. I got arrested and the feds showed up at her door. They wanted to know if she knew what I was up to—what they claimed I was up to."

"And she gave you up?"

"No." He was adamant. And frustrated. "That's what I'm trying to tell you. She lied, lied through her teeth. My sweet, church-going, God-fearing, preacher's wife of a sister swore up and down that she'd never heard of me being involved in political anything."

"So, you're saying the newspaper reports are all wrong. That she actually tried to protect you?"

"Oh, I admit she was trying to protect herself, too. But I didn't see nothing wrong with that. And I still don't. I didn't want her in trouble because of me."

"The feds, did they have evidence against her?"

"They had a letter she'd written me and it mentioned the money she was giving me."

"Did it say what the money was for?"

"No, and that was the problem. The fact that it didn't ..."

"Meant the feds could fill in the blank, twist it any way they wanted to."

"Exactly. So she ended up denying, not just any affiliation with the Party but to having anything to do *any* group or organization that pushed for Negro advancement or social equality."

"Denied your work? In a sense, denied you?"

"You mean like in Matthew 26:69-75? Peter and Jesus in the Garden of Gethsemane? Not quite. Because there, Peter was denying his god. I was not my sister's god and neither was the Party."

"Good point. And I see you know your Scriptures."

"Chapter and verse. Mama raised us to quote just as good as any preacher can."

"But you're not a church-goer."

"No, I left that nonsense behind a long time ago."

"Your feelings toward Levy: Is it because he's a preacher or is it just him, personally?"

"Both. Most of them are just a bunch of hypocrites."

"Not all. Some do fine work. They achieve a lot for the community."

"While lining their own pockets. Oh, there's a few good

ones. I'll grant you that. But too many are grifters. As for Levy, I know his type."

"And that is?"

"A suck-up accommodationist. From the same tree as Booker T."

"I would disagree."

"Of course, you would."

"Hear me out. Levy has fought tooth and nail to build a church that offers hope and comfort, that offers a place for people to rally. He fought in court to buy land, land for colored people to build on."

"For some colored. Not all. He's every bit as class-conscious as any white man. Look at the kind of folks sitting in those pews. It ain't poor people."

"It isn't all rich ones, either. But—" I raised a finger. "I take your point. Just do take mine. Levy has done good for Harlem. Whether you like him or not, admit that he's done good things. If you stopped by his church, then—"

"I've been there. Vera got me to go. I'll never go back."

"Oh?"

"Look, he doesn't like me any more than I like him. First of all, I don't believe in no white man's God. I told you that. Second, if I did, I wouldn't go to Levy's church to find Him. I'll never step foot in there again. To worship there means you've got to worship him. To swallow his interpretation of the Word, hook, line, and sinker. And I won't be a party to that."

His anger growing, he said, "He's the one who made her do it, you know. Deny me, deny herself. Look at what he'd given her, he said: a big house, a nice car, a fur coat, and a cabinet full of china. Because of him, she was rubbing shoulders with all the fine and better people. Did she really want to give it all up, lose it all? Did she actually mean to jump off a cliff and take him with her, just to save me?

When she couldn't save me, anyway? I made my bed, he said, so she should let me lie in it—alone."

"How do you know he told her that?"

"She told me."

In fact, I could well imagine Levy saying something like that. If he had, then, to be honest, I couldn't fault him for it. Martin Del Ray had made his choices. Why should Vera pay for them?

"And what did you say?"

"That I understood. That I forgave her. But I asked her whether she'd ever forgive herself. That was the real question. And I'm not sure she ever did."

"What about Levy? Was he there when they questioned her?"

"Yeah. And he was scared—"

"Well, of course. They both were—"

"The difference is, she was scared for me and for him. He was just scared for *himself*."

"You can't know that."

"I can. He was worried about how it would look if it got out that the preacher's wife was mixed up with a bunch of atheists, and that she might be arrested and charged with sedition. So he told those agents he'd forbidden—get this, *forbidden—his* wife from having anything to do with quote-unquote 'niggers who think they deserve the same rights as white folks.'"

"He didn't actually say that?"

"She said he did."

"And you think he meant it?"

"I do. She said he didn't. She said he told her that all he cared about was getting them agents out of the house. That whenever you get caught in a situation like that, you just tell them what they want to hear and move on."

"But you don't believe that was his motive?"

"*She* believed it, or certainly *wanted* to believe it, so I accepted it. Look, I didn't want my life to destroy hers. I mean, I don't like the man, but I won't deny that he gave her all the pretty dresses she ever wanted. We grew up dirt poor, so I could understand what that meant to her. It's just that ... in the end, he also demanded a price for it. And the price was just too damn high."

I let his words sink in, then thought of something else. "You said she was having an affair?"

"Yes."

"Did you tell the police that?"

"No."

"Why not? It might've deflected suspicion away from you."

"But it would've hurt her, damaged how people remember her."

An expression of love, of protectiveness. I admit it impressed me. "Do you think he might've had the same suspicions you did?"

"Who? Levy?"

"Yes."

"And hurt her?"

I nodded.

"Do you think that?" he asked.

"No, but I want your opinion."

He didn't answer.

"The police," I said, "are looking at everyone. They must've asked you that."

"They did."

"And what did you tell them?"

He was silent for several long seconds, then exhaled reluctantly. "I said ... that I didn't think he did it."

"No?"

"No. Look, he's a stuffed shirt. He wanted a pretty

woman. He got one. A smart, pretty woman. And he didn't know what to do with hr. But I don't think he'd have ever hurt her. Not that way. He loved her. As much as I dislike him, I won't deny that. As much as he can love anyone, he loved her. He truly did."

"Do you believe him?" Sam asked.

"Yeah," I nodded, still considering the matter. "I can't say why, but I do."

Sam heaved a deep sigh. "Well, you know what that means, where that leaves us. If you eliminate him as a suspect, then that leaves ..."

"Yeah, I know. Levy—him or the unknown lover."

"What if it is Levy? Are you ready to go down that road?"

I knew what Sam was alluding to. It was never easy to cover a case when you knew the suspects involved.

"Yes, I'm ready, " I said unhappily. "If I have to be, I will be."

Our gazes met.

"Okay, then," he said.

"Okay."

That evening I attended a social event at Lilly Stanford's house. Of course, all the conversation was about Vera's death. It turned out that a good number of people thought she'd been having an affair. More than a few found it titillating to play with the idea that Levy had found out about it and killed her—or had her killed. Of course, none of the suspicions were stated outright. People were much too polite to be direct about it. Instead, they were circumspect, letting meaningful eyebrows and heavy silences convey a sense of their true feelings.

I tuned out most of the speculation, but my ears perked up when I overheard what Ethel Jones had to say. She was a soft-spoken soprano, a plump woman with the voice of an angel. She was a librarian and worked with Ernestine Rose down at the 135th Street public library to run a literary salon for colored writers and their readers.

I bided my time until I could get her alone to speak with her. "Did you say you actually saw Vera the afternoon she died?"

"I sure did. She was getting into a man's car. Can you believe that? I actually saw them. Imagine that! Do you think he was the one? Why maybe she was trying to end it, you know, and he didn't want to let her. Maybe, he got angry, he killed her in a fit of passion, distraught at the thought that she was dropping him and going back to Levy. What do you think?"

"I think ... that if you saw something like that, then you should go to the police with it."

"Oh, no," she clutched her pearls. "I could never. I mean, well I did think about it, but I told Herman, and he said not to. He said it wouldn't be worth the trouble, that he didn't want me getting mixed up in something like that, something so sordid." She paused. "I mean, what do you think? You think I should talk to them, don't you, the police, I mean?"

"I think that if something were to happen to you and someone saw something that could help, then you'd want that person to speak up, wouldn't you? And that Herman would want them to help find the person who harmed you."

She mulled that one over. "It is one way of looking at it, isn't it?"

"The man. Did you recognize him?"

She drew her eyebrows together, thoughtful. "Hmm. Yes, actually, I think I did. The reverend used to have a man working for him who looked just like him. I remember thinking it was him, and that's how she probably met him, when he was working in the church office."

"Did you say 'was'?"

"Yes. If he's the man I'm thinking of, then he used to help with the books, kept the accounts straight. But I don't think he's there anymore. I haven't seen him around."

"You wouldn't happen to know his name, would you?"

"No, indeed, I don't. But I can tell you what he looked like."

CHAPTER 8

The next morning, I climbed the stairs to Levy's church office and asked to see him. The place was almost as quiet as the church itself. The only sound came from the typing of the office secretary. Denise Brown was in her thirties and had a hard face with strong angles. No makeup, no jewelry, hair severely pulled back. Simple, monotone clothing. Monotone in every way. Professionally plain. It was impossible to tell whether this represented her true personality or whether it was calculated. Either way, it all projected the message that she was not to be trifled with.

"The reverend's not in this morning," she said when I identified myself. For all the cold hard exterior, she had a warm voice, made softer by the traces of a Georgia accent.

"Oh, that's too bad. Could you please tell him I stopped by?"

"Of course."

I gave her my name. "He'll know the reason for my visit."

She scribbled a note and nodded goodbye, head bent, her thoughts already elsewhere.

I took that for the dismissal it was meant to be, thanked her, and started out. Quite honestly, I had every intention of leaving, but I had taken only a couple of steps when a thought occurred to me. I paused and walked back to her desk.

She looked up. "Yes?"

"I was wondering whether you couldn't help me. Then I wouldn't have to bother the reverend," I paused, then added, "at a time like this."

It wasn't very subtle what I said and it wasn't meant to be.

She pressed her lips together unhappily, then plastered on a polite smile. "All right. If I can."

"I'm told that the reverend has a man working here, doing his accounting work."

Her eyebrows arched and her head canted to one side in an air of slight surprise. "Well, he doesn't right now, but he did."

"A mister ... ?"

"Mr. Slocum."

"Slocum?"

"Nate Slocum."

"Do you know where I could find him?"

She frowned. "Why, if you don't mind my asking, would you be looking for *him?*"

Clearly, I'd hit a sore spot. I started to say that I was looking for someone to help me with my taxes, not quite the truth but not a lie, either, but she didn't give me the chance.

"I recognize your name, you know. You're a reporter, right?"

"Yes, I—"

"If you're here to dig up dirt or pester the reverend about—well, about what happened to his wife, then—"

"I'm not. I was there when the reverend received the news. And yes, my paper is covering the investigation, but I'm here as a friend of the family."

That gave her pause. But only for a moment. "Well, if that's why you're here, then why are you asking about Mr. Slocum? What does one situation have to do with the other?"

"Situation? There's a situation with Mr. Slocum?"

She didn't answer. Not at first. Then she gave a tight-lipped reply. "As it happens, Mr. Slocum is no longer with us."

"What does that mean?"

"It means," she paused, "that the reverend fired him."

"*Fired* him? When?"

"About two weeks ago."

The implications were obvious. *Could it be that simple? That Levy had fired Slocum and Slocum had killed Vera in revenge?*

I knew what Sam would say. *But this could also point to Levy. If he found out that Slocum and Vera were—*

"Why'd he let him go?"

She picked up a sheaf of papers and gave them a hard bounce on her desk, while her fingers nimbly worked to line up the edges. "I'll be sure to tell the reverend you were here."

I leaned on her desk. "Look, you've said this much. You might as well spill the rest. Especially if it could possibly help find the man who did it."

She paused and looked up at me. "Do you actually think that what happened with Mr. Slocum, that it has to do with the murder?"

"I don't know. You tell me."

She opened her mouth, then closed it again. "I don't believe in gossiping."

"Gossip is when you tell second-hand stories, tall tales, and lies meant to hurt people. That's not what I'm asking of you."

She thought about it. Then shook her head. "I just can't. I can't have my name or nothing I say in the paper. I--"

"Whatever you tell me, it's off the record. I won't use your name. I won't say anything about you."

"But the reverend will guess. He'll—"

"I'll write it so that nobody knows what I got from where."

"You can do that?"

"It's part of my job."

She held on to her info for another ten seconds, then gave a relenting sigh. "All right. Fine. The reverend told Mr. Slocum that he did a poor job with the books. 'Messed them up' he said."

"You heard them?"

"I didn't mean to. I certainly wasn't eavesdropping, if that's what you're wondering. But it was hard not to hear them. They weren't keeping their voices down. They knew I was out here, but they didn't care. They were shouting and yelling. It got pretty heated in there."

So, no, Sam, not an affair. Not Levy. A professional reason for the firing, not a personal one. But one that had nothing to do with Vera.

"Had there been any signs of trouble before then?"

She shook her head. "Not to my knowledge."

"How did the reverend find out?"

"About the problem with the books? I don't know. One minute everything was fine and the two of them were getting along great. The next thing you know, they were having this big blow-up and the reverend wanted him out of here. Told him to 'git' or he'd phone the police."

"He said that?"

"He sure did. I ain't never seen him that angry. And afterward, that Mr. Slocum, he used to call up here, asking to talk to the reverend, and the reverend would ask me who was on the line, and if I said it was Mr. Slocum, the reverend would say to hang up."

"So, the reverend didn't take any of Mr. Slocum's calls?"

"Not to my knowledge."

"And when was the last time Mr. Slocum called?"

She wrinkled her forehead and was thoughtful. "I don't know. It's been a while."

"What's 'a while'?"

She shrugged. "Oh, maybe a few days. Not quite a week." She was losing interest in the conversation.

"One last question?" I said.

She looked unhappy but nodded.

"Was the reverend's wife present during the argument?"

"Between him and Mr. Slocum?" she frowned. "No. She didn't have nothing to do with it."

Maybe my question unnerved her. Maybe she thought I was accusing Vera of having done something wrong. I wasn't, but maybe she thought I was. A nervous look came over her face. I felt the shutters come back down.

"Look, I need to get back to work," she said. "I really do have a lot to do."

"Thanks. I appreciate your having spoken to me."

"And you won't print anything I said?"

"I give you my word."

She gave a curt little nod and went back to her papers, once more the efficient and discrete secretary.

I had turned to go when I noticed a photographic portrait of Levy and Vera hanging on one wall. I recognized it as the work of Andrew King, a talented photographer whose murder I'd recently covered. Andrew had also taken a photo of me and my late husband. It was the best picture I had of us, in fact.

That thought led to another: how often death had visited us.

Hamp, gone. Andrew, gone. Now, Vera, gone, too. It's as though we're all under some curse.

I tried to shake off the thought, but it had power. An icy chill ran down my spine and I gave in to a little shiver. I scolded myself for being silly. Told myself not to be superstitious. *Be grateful, instead. Grateful these photos were taken, that we have them to save the images of those we've loved and lost.*

I nodded toward the photo of Vera and Levy. "They were a lovely couple, weren't they?"

She glanced up at me, then followed my gaze to the photo. "Oh, that they were."

"And to be able to work as a team, like that. Many people can't do that—be together day and night, working together, living together. It's hard."

"Yes, it is." She swiveled in her desk chair to give the photo her full attention. Possibly she'd seen it so often, she didn't notice it anymore. But now, contemplating it, she gave a faint but very sad smile. "They were a good pair."

"Human, of course," I said, hoping she'd take the bait. "But nobody's perfect all the time."

She cocked her head. "Well, most of the time, yes. But lately," she scrunched up her mouth.

"Lately, what?"

"Do you promise not to use this?"

"In the paper? Of course, I do. We're just chatting you and me, like I said, off the record." I smiled to reassure her.

She bit her lip and frowned. "It's just this: it's as you say, the reverend and his missus, they were a good couple, but lately something wasn't quite right between them. Something was ... well, I can't quite put my finger on it. It was just ... different."

"Were they fighting?"

"Oh, no, nothing like that. It was more ... subtle. Something hidden. A tension that wasn't there before." She paused, then waved her hand in the air. "Never mind. It was probably just my imagination."

"I doubt that. You strike me as being very observant."

Her lips lifted in the briefest of smiles. "Thank you. Mama always did say I have a knack." The smile disappeared and the furrow between her eyebrows deepened. "Now, I really do have to get back to work."

"Thank you, again," I said and turned to go.

Could it really be this easy, this simple? I wondered. *Find Slocum and find the killer?* I certainly hoped so. *Not all cases have to be complicated. Not all have to be nightmares of uncertainty and investigation.*

"One other thing," she said.

I turned in the doorway, one hand on the knob. "Yes?"

"Mr. Slocum told the reverend that he was gonna fix him."

"Nate Slocum threatened the reverend?"

"He sure did. Said he'd fix him 'good and proper.'"

It was as if the universe was answering my question. *Could it really be this easy? That simple?*

Yes, it could.

CHAPTER 9

I made a quick trip back to the office and checked the city phone directory. It looked like Nate Slocum had a phone and that phone was down on West 126th Street.

The building housing the phone that belonged to Slocum turned out to be a six-story mid-rise. It was in good condition. Very good, actually. So good it was bordering on what you might call 'chic.'

A couple leaving the building sailed out and I sailed in behind them. The lobby was nice, but once I got to the upper floors, all the chic fell away. This was a building in decline.

Slocum's apartment was easy to find. I rapped on the door. There was no answer. I rapped again. The door next to his opened and a young woman stepped out. She was in her late twenties and wore a smart suit with a modest fur boa tossed casually over one shoulder. She saw me and flashed a smile. It was a nice smile, convivial even. Too bad it didn't match the look in her eyes. There was suspicion there. And more than a hint of jealousy.

"Oh, he's not home," she said sweetly, her gaze raking me up and down, measuring, comparing.

"Do you know when he'll be back?"

She closed her door, slid a key into the lock, and turned it. "Sorry. I have no idea. But I wouldn't hang around, waiting for him, if I were you."

"Why's that?"

"I think he's gone."

"You mean, moved out?"

"No, I'm not sure about that." She shrugged. "It's just that I haven't seen in him a while. It's been a few days, come to think about it."

"Oh," I said, adjusting my expectations—and waiting for her to leave. "Well, thank you," I said when she didn't.

"If you want to give me your name, write a note," she said, "I'd be happy to give it to him."

"That's all right. A note's a good idea, but I think I'll just slip it under his door."

The mask dropped for a split second, just long enough for me to see the ugly. Then she said, "Suit yourself," and gave a shrug of exaggerated indifference. She dropped the key into her purse and snapped it shut.

I dug into my purse, took out my steno pad and a pencil, flipped the pad open, and started scribbling.

"Well, it was nice meeting you," she said with a little good-bye wave and trotted away.

I stopped writing and watched her descend the stairs. I listened for the clack-clack-clack of her heels as headed to the front door, and finally heard the sound of the front door itself close. Just to make sure, I crept to the stair banister and peeped over it. No sign of her. Good. I slipped the pad and pencil back into my bag and dug out my lock-picking tools.

THE FOUL ODOR hit you the moment you walked in the door. Slocum's one-room apartment was a good size, though, bigger than most kitchenettes I'd seen. It had two windows overlooking the park. Not a bad view. And lots of light. At the moment, that light was mostly gray. It made for a rather cold atmosphere.

But, to be fair, everything about the place was cold. And somehow gray. And somehow like a prison cell. A very, very nice prison to be sure, but a prison nonetheless.

The furnishings were Spartan, strictly utilitarian. The bed was a narrow cot. Grayish white sheets; gray blanket. And so tightly made it looked as though you could bounce a dime on it. There was a bedside table with a lamp and a bible. A radio atop a small scarred black dresser. And a gray card table with one chair. Not a full kitchen. Just a stove and a sink recessed into the wall. No private toilet. But a bathtub that sat just off from the kitchen area.

The place was orderly. But it stunk, like days' old garbage. When I checked the sink, I found a cup of dried coffee, a bowl of congealed soup and the remains of a ham sandwich.. Mice had been at it. Their droppings were on the floor and the counter.

So much for chic.

I checked his closet. No coat or hat. Just one suit. Of middling quality, but clean, and well-cared for. Nothing in the pockets. Two ties, one black and one blue. And two white shirts, both slightly frayed at the collar and one with a lipstick stain. (The color not matching Vera's. Looking similar to the neighbor's, though.) And at the bottom of the closet, a pair of black leather shoes. Pretty decent quality. Polished. Also cared for.

A conservative man. Serious. With simple, perhaps even potentially sophisticated taste.

That was something Vera would've found attractive. In the abstract. But in reality? That was another question.

I knew I couldn't stay there for long. He might walk in the door any minute. But I couldn't bring myself to leave. I stood in the center of that barren little room, looking around, not knowing exactly what I was looking for. Maybe just something, anything to give me a deeper sense of the man who lived there. But there was nothing, nothing personal here. No pictures or knickknacks. No letters or newspapers.

The place was ... too clean. It spoke of a man who hides, conceals. Where was his heart? The key to who he was? I went back to the closet, checked the shelf above and the floor below. Nothing. I checked the dresser, pulling out drawers, then the sole cabinet over the kitchen sink. Searching for something, anything.

Find nothing.

I sagged down on the bed, no longer caring if I wrinkled it and left traces of my presence. The chippy next door would tell him I'd been here anyway.

I looked around, taking in my surroundings. It was impossible for any normal person to live in this barren an environment. There had to be ...

Hmm.

What about ...? I tapped the firm mattress beneath me. What about under the mattress? It was the classic hiding place for anything worth secreting. How could I have not thought of it before?

I stood up and started pressing my hands down on the mattress, feeling for bumps and finding plenty, but none of them hard or oddly shaped. Feeling increasingly foolish and frustrated, I dropped down to my knees and started shoving my right arm under the mattress. That got me absolutely nowhere.

Not until I saw what was under the bed.

"WHAT YOU FOUND, you did put it back, didn't you?" Sam asked.

"Of course, I did. I'm a snoop, not a thief."

Sam and I were sitting in his office, the door closed. I'd been in such a hurry to share the news of my discovery that I hadn't even bothered to take off my coat. I slipped out of it now, letting it slide into folds around my waist.

Sam leaned forward, his fingers steepled, pondering the news I'd brought him. "Five hundred smackeroos, huh?"

"To the dollar. I counted it twice."

"And tell me again, you found it where?"

"In a fake bible. The pages had been glued together and then the center hollowed out."

"Hmph-hmph-hmph. Such disrespect." Sam shook his head. I couldn't tell if he was serious or joking. "Big bills?" he asked.

"Nope. Small, dirty, and used."

"So, he didn't get the cash from a bank."

"I'm wondering whether he stole it."

"Embezzled it from Levy's church?"

"Yup."

"But if that's the case," Sam began. "If that's why Levy fired him, then why he didn't report him to the police?"

"He might've wanted to but he would've worried about the scandal. Respect and reputation—they're like currency to men like Levy. He had to claw and scratch his way to the top. He treasures respectability the way other men treasure gold. His very livelihood depends on his capacity to command respect. Even the whiff of dirty dealings could've cost him a whole lot more than however much Slocum stole."

"So, he just let him walk away?"

"Apparently. He just let him go. But it looks like Slocum wasn't interested in going anywhere."

"You mean what the secretary said?"

"According to her, Slocum wasn't about to let bygones be bygones."

"So, you think he killed Vera to retaliate against Levy?"

"It would fit."

"But why not kill Levy?"

"Because, to a certain kind of low-life, that wouldn't have been enough."

BLACKIE WAS on the phone when I walked in. He waved me to sit down. I gathered from his half of the phone conversation that he was getting a report from his dentist.

"That was my dentist," he said upon hanging up.

"I gathered."

"Says I got a big cavity."

"You need to get it fixed."

"Nah." He waved a hand. "It'll keep."

I raised an eyebrow but said nothing. I've seen bigger and tougher men than Blackie to quail at the very thought of sitting in the dentist's chair.

"How're your pearly whites doing?" he asked.

"Mighty fine, if I say so myself," I said and flashed a toothy grin to prove my point .

He gave a grunt. It said it all. "I take it you're here about the Kincaid case."

"Yup."

"Like I'm just supposed to hand over anything and everything I've got, to you, a reporter?"

"Come on, Blackie. You know I'll share. I always share."

He raised an eyebrow.

"Well, OK, almost always," I said.

"So, your appearance here today, it means you've come bearing gifts?"

"To share. Gifts to share. You show me yours and I'll show you mine."

"All right." He narrowed his eyes. "Let's share. You'll share yours, first. Then, maybe, I'll think about sharing mine."

I forced a smile. The fact was, Blackie and I needed one another. We undoubtedly had one of the oddest relationship in New York City law enforcement — a male white Irish cop sharing tips with a female colored reporter. Sometimes, it didn't work out so well, but most of the time, it did. It's just that every now and then Blackie felt the need to clarify just who was in charge. When that happened, I just had to grin and bear it.

I launched into a recital of the information about the accountant. Blackie listened politely for a couple of minutes, then held up his hand.

"If that's all you've got, then you've got nothing to exchange. I know about him already."

"Oh, do you?"

"A lady came in this morning, told me all about it, how she saw Vera Kincaid getting into the man's car and everything. She didn't give us his name but we were able to figure it out fast enough."

Now, it was my turn to narrow my eyes. "This lady, her name wouldn't happen to be Ethel Jones, now would it?"

He cocked his head. "And what if it was? Why? Is she not reliable.?"

"Oh, she's reliable, all right. As solid as Manhattan granite. But the only reason—and I do say 'only' reason—she came in here to talk to you was because she talked to me first and I convinced her to. So, you owe me for that one."

"Is that right? You wouldn't be trying to pull a fast one on me now, would you?"

"How else would I know it was her if I hadn't talk to her first? She told me she was reluctant to talk to the police because her husband was against it. Said he didn't want her mixed up in such a thing. I had a little chat with her and I guess whatever I said, it caused a change of heart. So, the I.O.U's is on you, Blackie."

"All right. All right. Sheesh! I shoulda known. Don't none of your people ever come into this station to volunteer nothing."

"You said she came in this morning?"

"Yeah."

"So you've had the information for a while. What've you got on him?"

"Nothing."

"Nothing?"

He shook his head. "The man's a ghost. There's a paper trail going back five years and then it stops. It's like he came out of nowhere. There's nothing on him. Not a thing."

Hmm. It was easy to start over in those days, to create a whole new identity. All you had to do was cross state lines and give yourself a new name. you could effectively disappear from one state to the other. Take on a new name. It was simple. The fact that he had a past, or rather a lack of one, indicated that he had something to hide.

"Well, surely that must move him up your suspect's list," I said.

"Oh, he's up there, all right. Not only does he have a disappearing past, but he's seems to have disappeared himself."

"You're telling me that there's no records of this man's existence prior to five years ago and that now he's also missing? Blackie, he was the last man seen with Vera."

"That's only the half of it. We went to his apartment and found at last five hundred dollars in cash."

I puckered my lips in the form of a whistle. "Any indication of where the money came from?"

He shook his head. "Not a one."

"Maybe he stole it from the church. Maybe those accounting irregularities were actually a matter of stealing."

He nodded. "It would fit."

BACK HOME THAT EVENING, I made a cup of tea, then curled up before the living room fire and settled down to think.

Nate Slocum. Levy's secretary said he'd fired Slocum because Slocum had 'messed up the books.' She hadn't mentioned any embezzlement or supposed affair between Slocum and Vera.

But she wouldn't have, of course, out of loyalty.

What was bothering me? I tapped my teaspoon against my lips. The problem was simple. Privately, I had jumped to the conclusion that her not mentioning an affair was proof that such an affair did not exist. And I'd done so because I didn't want it to. I didn't want to believe that Vera would do such a thing.

But who was I to judge her? Suppose she had been having an affair with Slocum? Her brother said he'd seen her with a man, their heads bent in intimate conversation, and Ethel Jones had identified that man as the church accountant. Could both have been wrong?

I took another sip of soup, then set the tea aside, frowning.

No matter how hard I tried, I just couldn't wrap my head around the idea that Vera would step out on Levy. I'd bring myself to the edge of accepting it—right up to the edge—then back away. It wasn't just that she loved Levy; she loved herself, respected herself too much to do something like that. It was even harder to believe that she would've gone with someone who might've even been stealing from her church.

Suppose Del Ray and Ethel were wrong, not in what they saw, but in how they interpreted it? We only had their suspicions that she'd been having an affair. Beyond that, we had nothing. No proof of anything—

You don't want to believe they're right, said an inner voice, one that sounded an awful lot like Sam's.

No, I don't, I answered. *It don't make sense. That's what it is. It just don't make no kinda sense.*

But if they weren't having an affair, Sam's voice prodded, *then why was she meeting up with him? Especially that last time. Why did she agree to go meet a man she knew her husband had fired? There's one obvious reason, right? She was having an affair with him and couldn't stay away.*

Then Ethel's voice chimed in: *Why maybe she was trying to end it, you know, and he didn't want to let her. Maybe, he got angry, killed her in a fit of passion.*

I rubbed the side of my face. If I could just bring myself to the point of accepting the possibility that Vera's was cheating, then I still had to ponder—

Or maybe, just maybe, Sam's voice broke in, *she didn't know about the embezzling, if that's what it was.*

But she must have, I thought automatically. *Levy would've told her.*

Would he? Sam's voice asked.

Why wouldn't he?

The question echoed in my mind. I gave my head a little shake. The thought that he wouldn't have told her that he'd fired Slocum—now that really made no sense. So, he had told her. He would have. He *must* have. And she'd gone to see Slocum anyway, knowing what she knew, that her husband had fired him.

Sounds like a woman in love to me, Sam's voice said.

Or a woman who was trying to end it, Ethel's voice said.

There's no proof, I reminded them both. *It's all supposition. All theory.*

Sam's voice went on. *Of course, if you admit to the possibility that she was having an affair, then you must ask whether Levy knew about it.*

A scene flashed before my eyes. Of Levy confronting her and she admitting to it. Of Levy demanding that she break it off, and her agreeing to do it, then deciding to meet with Slocum that one last time, to break the news to him in person.

And then, of course, the meeting itself ... it all going quite wrong.

I leaned my face into my hands and covered my eyes. Was I choosing to be blind? Refusing to see what was right before me?

Once again, Sam's voice came, this time not to challenge but comfort me. *It's OK, Lanie. It's OK to discover that you didn't know someone as well as you thought you did.*

Something else occurred to me, some thought that hovered on the edge of my thoughts. I reached for it, had almost gotten it, when the doorbell rang.

CHAPTER 10

I glanced at the clock on the mantle. It was after seven. *Who in the world would be knocking on my door at this time of night?* I got up, slipped to the window, and drew back the curtain. My visitor's identity surprised me. I dropped the curtain and hurried to let her in. She stepped inside with a cold gust of wind behind her.

"Miss Lanie, I'm sorry to bother you this time of night."

"No, that's fine, Beulah." I waved her in and closed the door. "Come in."

I led her into the living room and offered her something warm to drink, but she demurred.

"I'm not here to stay long," she said. "It's that I thought, well, I have something to show you."

"Oh?" I was curious. "Please," I gestured toward the other armchair, "take a seat."

She glanced at the chair, as if embarrassed and uncomfortable. Sitting down implied that she was my social equal. She had been taught that she was not. She perched carefully on the edge of the chair cushion, a compromise I suppose between actually making herself comfortable and refusing my invitation all together.

I settled in the chair opposite her. "So, what's ...?"

Her face became quite serious. "Mr. Levy, he's got me getting Miss Vera's things together. He's gonna donate him, I guess."

"Sounds like a good idea."

"I guess." She frowned. "This morning, I was going through Miss Vera's closet, taking out her dresses, you know, and laying them out. And then I got to take down her hat boxes. You know, she had them all in boxes up on a shelf in her closet."

"Yes?"

"Well, I found something. Letters." She paused, her expressive gaze sombre. "I know I shouldn't have looked at them, miss. I know that, but I can't say's I'm sorry I did. If I hadna looked, then I wouldna known what they are, how important they are."

"These letters. They're to Miss Vera?"

"Yes, ma'am."

"And they're all from the same person?"

She nodded gravely.

"And that person, who might it be?"

I practically held my breath, waiting for her to answer.

She parted her lips to respond, then hesitated. Instead of telling me, she opened her large clutch, reached in with white gloved hands and came out holding a packet of plain white envelopes held together by a pink ribbon. Mutely, she handed them to me.

They were plain in quality, not cheap but not expensive, either. And blank on the outside. No information as to the sender or the recipient, not even a name.

"There's no address," I said.

"They didn't arrive by post. A boy always brought them."

"The same boy?"

"No, a different one, every time."

So, an attempt to obscure the identity of the sender.

"Were you always there when the letters arrived?"

"I think so. I opened the door the first time. After that, she wouldn't let me open the door no more. Said I had enough to do and she could take care of that herself. So I didn't open the door to him, but when I heard that bell ring, I'd sometimes peep out the window. Even if I didn't, I could tell when she got one of them letters. She was always real quiet after that."

I felt the envelopes, rubbed my thumb across them. They were thin, nearly flat. So, whatever missives they contained must've been brief and to the point. All had already been sliced open. I regarded her thoughtfully. I didn't mean for my expression to be in any way accusative, but she must've read it that way.

"I'm sorry," she said. "I know it sounds like I was spying on her—maybe, I was—but I knew something wasn't right with her. I could feel it."

"And so you went looking for the letters?"

"Oh, I was telling the truth, ma'am. Mr. Levy, he does have met pulling all her things together for to give away, but yes'm, I was wondering if I'd come across those letters along the way. And I did."

"And now you're here with them."

"Yes."

"What would you like me to do with them?"

Her forehead puckered with worry. "I trust you, miss, to do what's right."

"Suppose I gave them to the police?"

84

She swallowed hard and said, "I guess ... if that's what you think is right, then ..."

It wasn't. I wasn't sure what I was going to do with the letters but giving them to the police wasn't it.

"I'll make sure they're treated with respect," I said.

"Please don't let 'em get splashed all over the papers," she said, "but do do something about them."

Splashed all over the papers.

No doubt this is what she feared would happen if the police got hold of them. Yet, here she was, giving them to me, a reporter. It seemed contradictory, on the face of it. But if you looked at it from another angle, I suppose, it made sense, an intuitive, instinctive kind of sense. She was trying to get ahead of the story, to control it by controlling who knew what and when they knew it.

But just in case she didn't know what I did for a living, though I could hardly think how that was possible, I said, "You do know that I work for a newspaper?"

"Oh, yes'm. I do. I also know that you were one of Miss Vera's dearest friends. Maybe, you didn't see each other all that often, but I heard her say she always knew you were there for her. She thought of you like a sister."

I reached out and squeezed her hand. "Thank you."

Kind words, meant kindly, but they provoked a wave of guilt. I should've made more time to see Vera. I should've been there when she needed me.

I was curious about something. "You didn't consider giving them to the reverend? After all, he is—"

"No, miss. You can't do that—"

"Oh, I won't," I said quickly. "It just strikes me that you didn't."

She dropped her gaze, then after a moment nodded. "I'm sorry, miss, but I didn't want to see him hurt no more. He ain't been the same since it happened."

PERSIA WALKER

"Of course."

She dug a handkerchief out of her purse and dabbed her eyes. "You know, something went wrong in that house. It even before Miss Vera died. I could feel it."

"Oh?" I edged forward. "What makes you think that?"

"It was Miss Vera. She was selling her clothes, pawning her jewelry, anything and everything she didn't think the reverend would notice. And she told me she was going to cut down on my days, said she would help me find work somewhere else."

I now remembered Vera having asked me if I needed help. The question had seemed to come out of the blue.

"When did she first say this?"

"About a week ago." She kneaded her handkerchief. "I'm pretty sure she'd already pawned some of her jewelry." Her eyebrows shot up. "Good Lord! I almost forgot." She went into her bag and pulled out a slip of paper. She handed it to me and I turned it over.

"B. Berkowitz. Cooper Square Loan Office," it said, and it had an address on it, 15 Cooper Square. Downtown. Not in Harlem. Nowhere near it. Far away from any place where someone was likely to recognize her.

A pawn ticket.

With a date on it. The day before she died.

CHAPTER 11

S he left soon after that. Minutes later, Sam arrived. I hadn't expected him to stop by that evening, but I was glad he did. As usual, he came bearing groceries, and after giving me a quick but loving kiss, took over what was fast becoming his sovereign domain in my house: the kitchen.

Our relationship had settled into something of a routine. I was far more at ease with it than before. I can't cook a lick, so Sam often put me to work on some minor tasks. But that evening, I settled myself at the kitchen table with a second cup of tea and the notes Beulah had brought.

"What are those?" He paused while seasoning the ground beef for the meatballs to his spaghetti. A simple dish, but Sam did something wonderful with the seasoning that elevated the dish above the ordinary and everyday.

"Letters," I said. "Between Vera ... and the man who may have killed her."

My words had their desired effect.

He froze, one hand paused in sprinkling the oregano. "And you're telling me now?"

"I would've said something sooner, but you didn't give me a chance. You said you were hungry and wanted to get down to cooking."

"Well, I'm listening now. Talk to me."

"Vera's housekeeper just brought them.."

He went back to seasoning. "Read them out loud."

I removed the sheets from their envelopes. The missives were written in a rough penmanship. They weren't even dated. But I thought I could ascertain the order in which they'd been sent by their content.

"'I will tell,'" I said, reading from the first. "'I will tell them all what we did together, what you let me do to you.'"

"Hmph," Sam grunted. "He wasn't playing around."

"No, I'm afraid not." I drew my fingertips down the page. "He names a price. Two hundred and fifty dollars."

"He mention a meeting place?"

I shook my head.

"And that's the first one?" Sam said.

"Yes, I'm pretty sure it is. Because of what the next one says." I took it up. "'You should've been there. Now the price is five hundred.'"

"So, she stood him up," Sam said.

"Sounds like it." I took out the third and final one. "I'm assuming they were also communicating by phone. I mean, none of these notes mentions a time or place for a meeting."

He nodded, "Read on," his strong hands forming the ground beef into round balls that he would soon place in a frying pan.

"It contains another threat: 'Don't be short again. Bring it in full, or else I will tell,'" I read. "And he underscored the word 'will.' 'I will tell,' and 'then everyone will know what you truly are.'"

Sam sighed and shook his head. "I'm sorry, Lanie. I know you believed in her but—"

"I know it sounds unreasonable but somehow I still do."

"It's pretty clear from the letters—"

"I know. I know—"

"She had an affair and tried to break it off. So, he got angry and started blackmailing her. It also helps explain the cash. If he didn't embezzle it from the church, then he probably got it from her."

I nodded grimly and told him what Beulah had said about Vera selling her clothes and jewelry.

"Well, then." He applied oil to the frying pan, slid in the meatballs, and covered them with a lid. "But you know," he said, "they don't actually prove that this guy, this fired accountant, killed her. If anything, they might point to the opposite."

"How?"

"The fact is, either one of them—the husband or the lover—could've done it. The husband in jealousy. The lover in resentment and anger."

I stayed silent.

"Furthermore," Sam went on. "It wouldn't make sense for the thief to kill the goose that was laying the golden egg. I'm not saying it couldn't happen, but it's far more likely that the husband would lose his temper over it, and—"

"You're assuming that Levy knew about the notes." I told him what Beulah had said, about Vera always being careful to intercept the missives at the door.

"That doesn't mean Levy didn't know about them. He may have found them without Vera knowing about it."

"True." I rubbed my forehead. "It's just that ... the thought of Levy ... I can't imagine him hurting a fly. He's a stuffed shirt, for sure, but underneath all that, he's one of the gentlest people I know. And they were happy together."

"You thought they were."

I let out a deep sigh. "Yes, I guess ... maybe I was just seeing what I wanted to see."

"More likely, what *they* wanted you to see. A fine, upstanding couple like that. They hide their dirty laundry. You know that. They keep their ship trimmed neat and tight."

I didn't answer him. The likelihood was that he was right, but it was so hard to believe. "Vera was ... Well, she wasn't just one of the kindest, most generous people I know. She was also one of the most decent and honest. I just can't see her taking part in the hypocrisy, the mendacity, of an affair."

Sam looked at me and just shook his head. "Come on, baby. Why don't you take responsibility for turning the meatballs—"

"For doing what?"

"*Turning the meatballs.* You don't think they gonna turn themselves, now do you?'

When I didn't move, he gestured with his spatula. "Come on."

"You can't be serious."

"You wanna eat? You gotta work for it."

"Hmph."

I finished my tea, set the cup down, and sashayed over to his side. He comforted me with a hug and a kiss on the forehead.

Dinner was a quiet affair. Later, that night, curled up next to him in bed, he kissed my shoulder and whispered, "What're you thinking about?"

"Secrets," I said. "The many secrets that can plague a marriage and how dangerous they can be."

I wondered if he was thinking, wondering whether there had been secrets between me and my husband, Hamp.

"Yes," I said, answering what I assumed to be his unspoken question. "Hamp and I, we had our secrets, too." I paused, then said, "Well, at least, he did."

Sam brushed his thumb across my cheek. It came away damp and I realized that a tear had slipped from my eye.

"Shhh," he said. "You don't have to tell me."

"But I want to."

I drew a deep breath. "You know how he died, right? Fell down dead on a street corner, surrounded by strangers. Probably gone before he hit the ground."

I closed my eyes, but the moment I did, memories of that day, never far away, came flooding back. I opened my eyes and sought to fix my gaze elsewhere. It came to rest on a small statuette on the fireplace mantle. Not a good choice. The statuette was of a unicorn, made of black glass, fine and delicate. The sight of it brought back that day when Hamp and I had visited the island of Murano. We were on our honeymoon in Venice.

Our honeymoon, when we were so in love. I thought we had years, decades, before us.

I turned and pushed myself up, into a sitting position, and drew up my knees. "He knew," I said. "He knew, had known for a long time, that he had a heart condition, one that could kill him. He knew our time together could be cut short at any moment. Yet, he'd never told me."

"Lanie ..."

"Instead, he let me dream. He bought me this townhouse, talked about how we would fill it with children. All the time knowing, yet saying nothing."

Sam sighed. "Honey, I'm not going to say you're wrong for feeling the way you do, but ..."

"But what?"

"But maybe you could think about it from his point of view."

"I have.

"And?"

"It just makes me angrier."

"He probably didn't want you worrying about him, 'cause you know you would've. You're one of the most worrying women I know."

He smiled and gently brushed his fingertips under my lips. He was trying to make me smile. I refused to.

"I know he thought he could take care of it himself," I said. "I know all that. But I still think it was wrong."

"If it had been the other way around, what would you have done?"

Tears clouded my vision. I stopped seeing that horse, stopped seeing anything but the wall of pain.

"I would've told him. I wouldn't have wanted to. But I would've thought he had a right to know."

Sam was silent for a long time. Then he reached up, put his arms around me, drew me down, and hugged me. "Forgive him. Forgive *yourself.*"

"Myself? For what?"

"For not doing all the things you think should've done, would've done, if you'd known."

I didn't have an answer for that. Sam had put his finger on it.

"If I'd known ..." I began, my voice suddenly hoarse.

"If you'd known, then what? What would you have done differently?"

I didn't need to think about that one. "I would've told him I loved him. Every damn day."

"I think he knew that, Lanie. I surely do."

I twisted around and gazed at him. "How can you do that, Sam?"

"Do what?" He caressed my hair.

"Lay here and listen to me talk about him."

"Why shouldn't I?"

I searched for the right words for what I wanted to say. "Some men would be jealous."

Sam let out a chuckle. "Well, I'm not 'some men.'"

"No, you most certainly are not."

"Furthermore, why in the world would I be jealous?" His voice became serious. "He's gone, Lanie, and it's me who's here, lying here next to you. I know you loved him, but ... Well, crazy as it sounds, it's the fact that you could love so deep that makes me love you more."

"And you're not worried about me loving you?"

He cocked an eyebrow. "Should I be?"

"No." I shook my head and snuggled down next to him. "No, you needn't worry about that at all."

He lifted my chin and gave me a soft loving kiss. "I'm here with you, and I'm not going nowhere, not until—or unless—you tell me to go. Understand?"

I searched his eyes. He meant it.

But Hamp, he'd meant it, too, when he talked about a long life together. He'd meant it, too.

Sam reached over my head and turned off the bedside lamp. The room fell into darkness, lit only by the rays of moonlight streaming through our bedroom window.

"Promise me one thing, Sam."

"Hmm?" He rubbed his cheek against mine and kissed my earlobe.

"Promise you won't keep any secrets from me," I said. "Will you promise me that? If you have a problem or get into trouble, you'll talk to me about it?"

He paused and for an eternal moment, there was stillness. Then I heard him, felt his strong hands caress my breasts, felt him grow hard against my hip, as he led me into the dance.

It was only later, as he lay sleeping beside me, that I realized he'd never answered my last question.

CHAPTER 12

The next morning I went to the pawnshop. No. 15 Cooper Square turned out to be a three-story brick building near the intersection of the Bowery, Third and Fourth Avenues, and Astor Place. The front windows were full of items that people had parted with, lots of musical instruments (banjos, guitars, saxophones, and trumpets) on the left; jewelry on the right. I paused outside the window on the right. After a few minutes of searching, I saw an earring and necklace set I recognized.

The dealer was a frail, bent little white man with a big mustache and monocle. I didn't expect him to be all that cooperative, but he was sympathetic and helpful when I explained the situation.

"I remember her," he said. "Nice lady. I'm sorry to hear what happened to her. It's always terrible when bad things happen to good people." He raised a finger. "Hold on a minute."

He shuffled off to a back room, flipping back a curtain. I could hear him rummaging around, muttering to himself.

Several minutes later, he emerged from the back, like a wizened dwarf emerging from a cave, carrying an open book.

"Here," he said, "I found it." He laid the open ledger on the countertop. "This was the day, right?"

I twisted my neck a bit to get a closer look and he obligingly turned the book in my direction. "Yes, that was it."

"She brought in several pieces."

"Could I see them, please?"

"I'm sorry, but they're gone. All except a necklace and earring set."

"The one in the window?"

He nodded and told me what he'd paid her for it. I'd say it was less than half of what Levy had spent on it. The dealer asked me if I'd like to reclaim it. I actually hadn't thought about it beforehand, but at the question, I found myself saying, "Yes, I will."

BACK AT MY DESK, I put in a call to Levy at his church office.

"Good morning," I said.

"Lanie! How are you?"

It was only fair to him to get his comment before I wrote the story about Vera's murder—and the possibility, the suspicion, that she had been having an affair.

I was still unsure about what to do with the letters and whether to mention them. Sam and I had argued over the matter.

I'm not going to write about those letters, Sam. I'd be betraying a trust. It would be like stabbing Vera in the back. It would damage her reputation and wound those who loved her. It wouldn't be fair, Sam, with her not here to defend herself.

"Do you honestly think that by keeping it a secret, you'd be doing her a favor? You wouldn't be protecting her. But I'll tell you who you could be protecting—her killer. Do you want to do that, Lanie? Do you even want to take a chance *on doing that?"*

"Lanie?"

It was Levy. For a moment there, I'd drifted away, remembering the exchange with Sam, what was said—and what was not.

Secrets.

"So, do you have news for me?" Levy asked.

"News? Yes. I've been going over my notes, and I ... well, I thought you should know that I've uncovered some information, some indications that possibly could be construed to imply ..."

"Yes?"

I took a deep breath, then plowed ahead. "That could be taken to mean that Vera was having an affair."

There was an unholy silence. I heard Levy gasp, then nothing. He was holding his breath, as I was holding mine.

"Y-you must be m-mistaken," he said.

I didn't answer.

More silence, then: "You're sure? Absolutely sure? You have proof that my wife, my Vera, was cheating on me?"

I dodged the question of proof and asked, "Did you know?"

"Of course not," he said gruffly. "But look here, do you have proof? I mean, what's the basis for—?"

"Correspondence."

Another shocked silence. *So, he didn't know,* I thought. But then, deep down, a voice answered: *Yes, he was caught unawares. But is it the shock of a man who learns he's been deceived or of one who learns that others have found out?*

"From her to him?" he asked finally.

"From him to her."

I could sense him thinking.

"How did you come about these ... letters?"

"Is this why you fired him?"

"Fired him? Fired *who?*" His voice conveyed genuine puzzlement. Then came another gasp as he understood, put two and two together. "Oh, my—*NO!*" The words exploded out of him. "Do you mean to say you think that —?" He sputtered. "When you say fired, do you mean—you don't mean, you *can't* mean—that *Godforsaken accountant?!*"

"Slocum," I said. "Nate Slocum."

His voice was hard with rage. "You think Vera, my lovely dignified Vera, would debase herself with that swine, would get down in the dirt with that piece of shit?"

He went on like that for a while, a good long while. I didn't argue; I didn't say a word. I was tempted to hold the receiver away from my ear. But I forced myself to listen. He had every right to be angry. Every right to be hurt. I had been the messenger of some very bad news. And with my questions, I had not only slid in the knife but twisted it. As I sat listening to him, I knew that I was listening to the cries of a man in pain, a man who'd loved her as much as I thought she'd loved him.

"Slocum," I repeated when Levy had finally calmed down. "You did fire him, yes?"

He paused. The trust was gone. He wasn't going to answer my questions as readily as he one might've.

"Yes, I did," he said in a voice still tight w?ith anger.

"May I ask why?"

Another long silence. "Is this why you came here, looking for me? To accuse me, snoop on me?"

"I was there to find the truth, just as I'm trying to do now. So, please tell me. Why did you fire him?"

"It wasn't because he was having an affair with my wife, if that's what you want to know."

"Why then?"

"He messed up our billing and invoicing." Levy paused, then added with bitterness. "He might've even been stealing on the side. I can't say for certain, but I suspect it was headed in that direction."

"So, this had nothing to do with Vera?"

"My firing him? No, nothing. She had nothing to do with it."

"When did you let him go?"

"About two weeks ago."

"And since then?"

"Since then what?"

"Any communication from him?"

"Of course not. I told him if he ever showed his face again, I'd have him arrested."

"He never reached out to you?"

"Oh, he tried. He called me here a few times. I refused to speak to him."

That jived with what his secretary said. "The thing is, there's a possibility that this man was blackmailing Vera. She might've tried to end it and he—"

"Lanie, I'm telling you, no. My Vera wouldn't have—"

"She was selling her things, Levy. Emptying her jewelry box. She pawned an earring and necklace set. I talked to the pawn dealer myself and got it back from him. I—"

"That can't be. That just can't be."

"I'm sorry, Levy, but it's true. I have the jewelry right here."

"And you're sure it's Vera's?"

I described the pieces to him.

"I can't believe it," he whispered. "There must be some other explanation."

"What other one could there be?"

"I-I don't know."

I used the pencil to make notes.

"These letters," Levy said. "You're not going to mention them in your article, are you? Publish them?"

I took a moment to answer. "It's not up to me.. I won't be the one to make that final decision."

"Who will then?"

"My editor."

"Well, let me speak to him."

"I can't. He's ..." I looked up at Sam's office. He was hard at work on something, stacks of pages towering on either side of him. "He's not here at the moment."

I turned away and spoke into the phone. "Levy, don't worry. I-I loved Vera, too."

"Well, you don't act like it."

"I promise—" I bit my lip. "I promise to do everything I can to protect her memory."

He didn't say anything, but I could sense him thinking, pondering.

"I want to see the letters," he said.

"No, I'm afraid not."

"Why not? If they were from that man—that Slocum— from him to her, then they were her letters. That means, that as her husband, they're now mine."

"I told you, Levy. I'll protect her."

"I'm warning you," he said. "If I see those letters in your paper. If I see even the merest hint of scandal in your reporting on my wife, I'll find a way ... to take away your voice. If you use your voice to hurt my Vera, I'll use mine to take away yours. Every Sunday, in the pulpit, I will raise my voice against those who would seek to make money off of her death."

"Levy, that's not me."

"She loved you, Lanie, like a sister. I didn't think you'd be among those who would dance on her grave—"

"Levy, I—"

The next sound was the clink of the phone. He'd hung up.

CHAPTER 13

I t was only mid-morning and I already felt exhausted. The conversation with Levy had drained me. *How in the world did it go off the rails so fast?*

I told myself I should've known better. I should've known how he would react and handled it better.

I gave my head a little shake, massaged my temples, and went back to work, writing out my notes while they were still fresh in my mind. It took another twenty minutes, but then I had fully laid out everything so far and carefully put both the notes and the letters in a folder. I slipped it into one of the desk drawers and locked it. I was about to put the key in my purse when the phone on my desk rang.

"Lanie's World," I answered, using the name of my newspaper column.

"It's Blackie."

"Oh, good morning," I said, somewhat surprised that he would be calling me. Usually, it was me calling him.

"Just a courtesy call," he said. "Wanted you to know that I've confirmed the brother's alibi."

"The husband, too? Or just the brother?"

"The husband, too."

"Well, that's news. Thank you." I picked up a pencil and began tapping it on the desktop. "Any news on Slocum?"

"Still no sign of him." Blackie cleared his throat.

There was something he wasn't telling me. "What's going on, Blackie? You holding out on me?"

He paused. "Let's just say we're working another angle."

"You want to tell me about it?"

"Not at this time, no."

I hung up, thoughtful, and sat there holding the receiver. The wrinkles on my forehead were getting deeper by the second. *Now, what was* that *all about?*

I sat back in my chair, ran through everything I knew about the case, trying to figure out what 'new angle' Blackie might've stumbled upon. Only one name came to mind. *Slocum.* It had to be him. He was the only person I could think of, the *only* one, who might possibly have gotten Blackie to exclude both Levy *and* Martin from his list of suspects: Slocum. He was the man of mystery. So, he must be it. He had to be.

I happened to glance up and see Sam in his office. He had gotten up from his desk, from behind those stacks of papers, and was now standing in front of his wall map, staring at it, arms folded across his chest, his face scrunched up in an expression of deep thought.

I sauntered down to his office, stepped just inside the door, and rapped on the doorframe. "A penny for your thoughts?"

He tapped his lips with a forefinger, raised an eyebrow then pointed to the map. It was a map of Manhattan. But it extended as far north as the Bronx. "They never did figure out where Vera went into the water, did they?"

"No," I said, entering and joining him at the map.

"You know, I used to be a sports reporter. Used to cover the races up the Harlem River."

"No, I didn't realize." I glanced at the map. "So, I guess you'd know something about currents."

"A little something, yeah." He pointed to the northern stretch of Manhattan. "I'm thinking," he said slowly," that given the time of her death, the approximate time of it, and where she ended up, that she went into the water ..." He leaned forward and traced a circle on the map with an index finger. "Right there."

I examined the place he was pointing to, then turned to him and said, "So what are we waiting for?"

IT TURNS out we indeed have to wait a while. Sam had meetings and stacks of copy to edit on deadline. Meanwhile, I worked on a draft of my column and an article on the Kincaid story.

We finally set out in late afternoon. It was a cool day, with crisp air and a gray sky overhead. Sam and I made good time heading north. It only took us thirty minutes or so to reach our destination, the area that Sam had traced on the map. During the ride up, I filled Sam in on what Blackie told me in that last phone call."Well, it certainly sounds as though he thinks he's made a breakthrough," Sam said.

"He wouldn't tell me anything about it."

Sam chuckled. "Just think of it as a compliment, Lanie. He knew that if he gave you the slightest inkling of what he's up to, of what he's found, that you'd run with it. And not just run with it but probably get there before him. Shucks, baby, you got that cop running scared!"

We both laughed at the very thought.

"We're almost there," Sam said.

The Bronx Kill. *What an appropriate name,* I thought, *if this is where it happened.*

The Kill was a tidal strait that linked the Harlem River and the upper East River. It wasn't all that wide, but it could go deep and it was given to strong, turbulent currents.

"There's a stream—Mill Brook—that feeds into the Kill," Sam said, "and there's a railroad bridge that spans it. If she was killed and thrown into Mill Brook, then the tide would've carried her to where she was found."

Soon, we were trundling through a small park. It was getting dark by then. The place was quiet and isolated. The sounds of the city seemed far away.

"It's the perfect setup for lovers who want to meet in secret," Sam said.

"Or for a blackmailer to meet his victim and collect his payment." I gave in to a little shiver.

We turned onto a small road.

"Look!" I leaned forward, pointing.

A black car stood on the grassy area off under a small copse of trees. The car listed to one side as if it had a flat tire and the front passenger door stood wide open.

Sam and I glanced at each other. He slowed down and we silently drove past it. The window on the driver's side had been shattered, with sharp irregular bits of glass still jutting up from the steel frame. What appeared to be a male figure sat slumped behind the steering wheel.

"Pull over, Sam. Pull over."

Sam steered his car to the side of the road, half on, half off the grass, just ahead of the parked vehicle. "Do you recognize it?"

"I just know it's not Vera's."

We approached the driver's side. Sam had served in the

war and I'd covered a good number of homicide scenes, so we were both experienced in viewing the results of violence, but we'd never grown numb to it.

There was indeed a man in the driver's seat. He was half-erect, half-keeled over. He was obviously dead, had been for a while from the looks of it. A bullet hole had carved a hole in the left side of his head.

"That shot," Sam said, "was up close and personal."

From the size of the hole, it had been of fairly large caliber. I didn't need to see the other side of his head to know there probably wasn't much left of it. A bullet that made an entry hole that big would explode out the other side.

I swallowed, hardening my stomach. It wasn't easy to make out his facial features, not in the shadow of his car and not with all that blood. Even so, something about his face seemed vaguely familiar. Maybe it was just the profile. But no, I shook my head, that wasn't it. There was something familiar about him. I couldn't put my finger on it.

"Looks like he's alone," I said, "but there's something on the passenger seat." I walked around to the passenger side, bent down, and peered in. "Sam."

"You've found something?"

I beckoned for him to come around. When he joined me, I pointed to inside the car. A woman's scarf lay on the passenger seat. It had a pattern of lavender flowers and green leaves on a background of ivory. From the looks of it, it was made of silk.

"Vera's?" Sam asked.

"It looks like one I gave her. Levy said she was wearing it."

Sam straightened up and glanced around, taking in the whole scene. "The killer must have walked up to the driver's side first. Walked straight up to it. Cause this wasn't a drive-by. This car wasn't sprayed. The killer just walked up to the window, cool as you please, aimed, and fired. A precision hit."

"And Vera, she must've been in the car with him, sitting here in the passenger seat. She managed to get the door open and tried to make a run for it—"

"But she didn't get far."

Sam and I walked the short remaining distance to the bridge. Together, we looked over the edge to the rushing water below.

"The killer followed her," he said, "shot her in the back, and then ..."

"Tipped her over."

He turned to me. "You think she was the target? Or just happened to be at the wrong place at the wrong time?"

"Not sure," I said. "But I do think one thing's clear."

"What's that?"

"We just found Blackie's missing man, Nate Slocum."

I STAYED with the car while Sam went to find a phone and call Blackie. Sam was back pretty quickly, but it took Blackie another hour to get there. In the meantime, uniformed police from the local station arrived on the scene—and immediately began treating Sam and me as though we were the ones who'd pulled the trigger.

They had actually pulled out the handcuffs and were about to slap them on us when Blackie finally arrived. I must say he took his sweet time, examining the car, listening to the local lieutenant's report, including all of its innuendos and false assumptions, before sauntering over to speak to us, where we stood under police observation by one of the patrol cars.

"You *are* going to tell them we didn't do it?" I asked.

"I don't know," he said with an open-palmed shrug. "Should I? Did you?"

"Of course, not," I said, tapping my foot with annoyance.

"You told the lieutenant over there that you recognized the woman's scarf as belonging to Vera Kincaid? Does that mean you recognized the man, too?"

"I'm guessing it's Nate Slocum. But you already know that, right? I mean, I saw your guys going through his pockets and pulling out a wallet."

Blackie's dark brows drew together. "Yeah, it's him. How'd you know he'd be here?"

"We didn't."

"Then what are you doing here?"

I nodded toward Sam. "He figured it out."

"Figured what out?"

Sam explained it as he'd explained it to me.

"So," Blackie said, "a lucky guess, then."

"No," Sam said, "an educated one."

Blackie looked sour. He looked at me to see if I had anything to add and I nodded toward Sam. "It's what he said."

Blackie gave Sam a gimlet eye, then turned back to me. "Look, I know you don't want to hear this, but—"

"Lieutenant!" There was a cry. "Lieutenant, over here!"

We three looked around, then realized that the voice was coming from under the bridge. We hurried to the railing and looked down. A couple of officers stood on an embankment at the river's edge, waving up at us. They had found something.

It turned out to be an abandoned tent and fishing

tackle. There was an old tin pot, the cold dead ashes of a fire, and a tin plate with food still on it.

"Looks like someone was living here till recently," Blackie said.

"Yeah, but he cleared out fast," Sam said.

"Wonder why," I said.

Sam pointed to the tin pot. A bullet had pierced it through and through. "I imagine that's why," he said, then looked upward toward the bridge. We had a clear view of it from where we were standing.

"Whoever was here," Sam said, "would've been able to see what happened—see the face of the man who did it."

"And the killer," I said, "he would've been able to see whoever was standing here, too."

Blackie and Sam turned to me, realization in their eyes. We had a witness—and a killer who was out to get him.

CHAPTER 14

I t was dark by the time we got back to the office. The staff had gone home and the empty newsroom, cavernous with its high ceilings, seemed ghostly. But it was still warm. I appreciated that. It had been cold in Sam's car on the drive back. I'd sat there shivering for most of the drive.

As soon as we got back, I headed downstairs to the newspaper morgue, where we kept copies of old newspapers. It didn't take anywhere near as long as I thought it would to find what I was looking for.

Thirty minutes later I was back at my desk, reviewing my notes. They were on Slocum. He'd looked familiar and now I knew why. Five years earlier, he'd gone by the name of Chiles, Mason Lou Chiles, and he was working for a loan shark, a pretty bad one, the kind who nursed grudges.

After several minutes, I reached for the phone, had a couple of calls put through, not to anyone official but to people who were still in the know, and got the info I needed. Then I sat there for a while, cogitating. Was this the new angle Blackie had alluded to?

I was about to place another call, this time to the homicide cop, when Sam walked up.

"I think I've found the witness," he said. "At least, I know where to look. Let's go."

I glanced out the soot-covered windows of the newsroom. It was pitch-black outside. And cold, too. Just looking at it made me shiver. A sense of exhaustion hit me. The only decent reason for going back out there was to go home. All I wanted to do was curl up in my nice warm bed, not traipse around in the dark, looking for a man who didn't want to be found.

"Now? Tonight?" I said.

"The sooner, the better."

On our way out there, I told Sam about Slocum and his links to a loan shark.

"Sam Sharkey's lowdown enough to have ordered the hit," Sam said. "The question is why. We know why he'd have gone after Slocum. But why kill a preacher's wife?" He took his eyes off the road a moment to glance at me. "You think she borrowed money from him and couldn't pay it back?"

"Highly unlikely."

"Well, so was her ending up where she did."

I didn't have an answer for that, so I said nothing and we rode the rest of the way in silence.

THERE WERE places in New York where Edison or Ma Bell or Consolidated didn't dare to tread. Places where you wouldn't find electrical wiring or telephone or gas lines. Places out of time. It was to one of those places Sam took me.

"I thought I knew this city," I said.

"But you didn't know about *this.*"

We were standing on the harsh rocky banks of a dirty waterway at the northern tip of Manhattan. Before us lay a rough and impoverished replica of Venice. Instead of Italian palatial buildings, you had shacks on stilts; instead of gondolas, dories tethered to rickety plank piers, and instead of blue-green canals, you had alleyways of gray and brown water that lapped in-between and ran underneath.

It was cold. As a matter of fact, it felt downright icy with an arctic wind blowing across the river. I turned up my coat collar, tucked my nose in the warmth of its fur, and hugged myself. "Where exactly *are* we?"

"Not far from where we found the car. Creeks run all around here, heading west. They run from the East River to The Bronx. Right now, we're at West Farms Creek. This one and Westchester Creek? Lots of folks call them home, living in shacks and moored barges."

Hidden New York. Hidden New Yorkers. "How in the world did you find out about this place?"

"Every now and then, a body gets washed ashore. Every now and then, a reporter will do a story. But I know about it from back when I was covering sports."

"And the witness?"

"I suspect he's one of these people."

"So it's knocking on doors, is it? Will they talk?"

"Maybe. Maybe, not. They don't trust cops or reporters, but they distrust the cops more. That might just give us the edge we need."

"Why didn't we do this when we were up here before? Instead of driving all the way back to the city?"

He smiled. "Well, don't you sound grumpy?!"

"I've got reason to be." I did a little jig and stomped my feet, trying to keep the blood moving. My toes were already turning into ice cubes. "It's colder than a mother-in-law's kiss out here."

Sam hugged me and rubbed my arms. "I just didn't want Blackie's men dogging our heels. Now, they're gone and we can ask around in peace."

I still wasn't happy but I couldn't argue. "All right," I sighed. "Let's get going."

The first few doors we knocked on, the folks shut the doors in our faces. There were others who at least spoke to us just long enough to say they didn't know anything. Finally, though, there was one guy who listened with sympathy. He thought for a while, then said the fish and tackle equipment sounded like it belonged to a man named Jake Bromley and told us how to find Bromley's shack.

We followed the directions and soon found ourselves in front of a rather whimsical but practical setup. The shack wasn't so much a shack as the deckhouse of a boat that had been dragged ashore. A chimney jutted out of the roof like a jaunty hat. The owner had cleared out the rubbish, installed what was in the summer a small garden, and used salvaged wood to build a fence that enclosed the perimeter.

The owner of this creative little homestead turned out to be a slightly-built bow-legged man. He had a wrinkled and weatherbeaten face that was the color of a well-baked brown potato. Looked to be in his sixties. He wore a moth-eaten hat, turned down on the sides, a patched wool jacket, and torn coveralls over a yellowed white shirt underneath. He took off his hat with a small bow, very old-fashioned and gentlemanly, when he let us in.

And he had a little girl with him, a child of about six or seven with big liquid brown eyes and a button nose, her hair plaited into two thick stubby braids. She was thin but otherwise looked healthy. She was dressed like a farm girl in a pinafore apron dress. It was simple and clean, if patched and faded. She clutched a homemade cloth doll, holding it tightly under one arm.

"My grandbaby," Bromley said, introducing her with pride, one protective arm thrown around her shoulders. "We named her after her mama, Ruth. Ruthie Anne. But I call her Buttercup. 'Cause she my little buttercup." He bent and told the child, "Show the lady and gentleman here your manners. Show 'em like I taught you."

The little girl smiled shyly but curtsied. I smiled at her and, gentleman that he is, Sam gave her a courtly bow in return.

Grinning, Ruthie held her doll up for us to see. "This is Miss Dollie. My mama made her for me."

"She's very pretty," I said.

"Beautiful," Sam said.

The doll was a cute homemade concoction of scraps and leftovers: brown burlap for the skin, braided black yarn for the hair, and flowered cotton remnants for a dress. Yellow thread had been used to indicate long eyelashes, eyes and a button nose, and red thread used to outline a full mouth. Made with scraps and leftovers, yes. But also with a lot of love and care and attention.

"Miss Dollie goes everywhere with her," Bromley said. "She don't go nowhere without it."

"Her mother. She lives here, too?" Sam asked.

The light in Bromley's eyes dimmed. "No, she gone. The TB took her. Last year, it was. Round 'bout this time last year." He looked down at Ruthie and hugged her to him. "It's just us, me and my grandbaby."

"And her father?" Sam asked.

"Went over there to that white man's war. Didn't come back. I told him not to go. But he wouldn't listen. Said that by helping the fight over there, he was helping the one over here. That the white folk would see us just as brave and willing to fight as anybody." Bromley shook his head. "That was nonsense. I could've told him that. But he believed it. Wanted to believe it. Said he had to believe it. Had to have hope. He was a good man. But naive. My daughter sure missed him. And now, Ruthie Anne and me, we gets to miss 'em both. But we good. We all right, doing fine, ain't we, Ruthie Anne? We doing fine."

He smiled down at her and she beamed back up at him. For a split second, I suspect they forgot Sam and I were even there. The old man and his granddaughter were bound by a love and loss that could shut out the world, at least for a few precious moments, and let them briefly forget its ugliness.

Bromley bent and kissed the child on the top of her head. "Go on and play now. Let me talk to the gentleman and the lady. And when they gone, I'll read you a good-night story from the Bible."

"Or maybe I'll read *you* one," she said.

"Yup, that'd be even better."

"OK, grandpa," she said, waved to me and Sam, and then scampered off.

"She reads already?" I asked.

"She's right smart," Bromley said. "Her mama started teaching her. After my daughter died, Ruthie Anne just kept going, taught herself."

"Amazing," Sam said.

"Yes sir. That she is."

Ruthie Anne had climbed up to the top of the bunk bed, where she sat, legs swinging and holding a silent conversation with Miss Dollie. My gaze moved from her to roam over the rest of his place.

It consisted of one room. It resembled a hunter's cabin. He'd managed to make it airtight, so it was actually warm in there. He'd rigged a curtain to separate the space into sleeping and living room areas. Just then, the curtain was pushed back so the entire room was visible. It held the bare necessities: the narrow bunk bed where Ruthie Anne sat. The beds were fitted with gray sheets and thin blankets, precisely made, on even thinner mattresses on a sturdy wood frame. As for the rest, there was a side table bearing an oil lamp and a worn bible; a medium-sized wood table with two chairs; a pot-bellied cast-iron stove; two sturdy-looking wall shelves bearing tools, tin plates, and canned goods. The place was spartan but still somehow cozy. It felt like a home.

"You have a nice place," I said.

Bromley smiled. "Yeah, we lucky we found it."

Chalk and charcoal portraits, as well as drawings of wildlife and plants, dotted the walls. They were incredibly good. Startling even. The whimsy, the pain, the courage of his neighbors: it was all there, captured with vivid detail. Portrait after portrait of grizzled men and ravaged women, all of them with lined faces, faces worn by age and disappointment, all of them smiling, all of them with the light of life and wit in their eyes. All except one.

"You did these?" I asked.

"Yes, ma'am." He gave a little self-deprecating chuckle. "You know how it is. You come up here when you're young and you got all kinds of dreams. Why, you just sure you gonna set the world on fire. Then life happens."

You're so right, I thought.

Sam said, "I want to thank you for agreeing to talk to us."

"Well, I don't like reporters or cops, but you two seem all right."

Sam brought the conversation around to the reason we were there. Bromley was obviously scared by what he'd seen that day, but he was willing to talk.

"I'm down there fishing, when I hear a shot. I look up and hear this woman scream. Then there's another shot. And then there's this man—no, this woman. She come first. She come stumbling to the side of the bridge. I can see she's bleeding. Blood coming down her front, her chest. And then this man, he come up behind her, and she just like, falls down, and he picks her up. He picks her up and throws her over. Picked her up like she ain't weigh nothing. Just puts her over the side of that bridge and into the water."

Bromley stopped, his face taut. He gazed down at his hat, fingering the worn brim, but I had a feeling he wasn't seeing it. "I couldn't save her," he said after a while. "I looked to see if I could save her but she weren't moving, just floating face down in the water. I must've made some kind of noise, 'cause then—then I looked up and I seen him looking down. He was looking down right at me."

"You saw his face?" Sam asked.

"I saw his and he saw mine. He raised that gun and pointed it at me and started shooting. I skedaddled out of there. I heard him shooting behind me. Sounded like the shots hit the rocks and my pot." His hands shook. "I been here ever since. Been here, laying low, scared to stay in and scared to go out, scared he's gonna find me. Find us," he added, with a glance at Ruthie.

I pulled out a newspaper photo and showed it to Bromley. "Is this the man?"

Bromley peered at it, then shook his head. "No, ma'am. I'm sorry but that's not him."

I knew it was a long shot, but I'd be lying if I said I wasn't disappointed at Bromley's response. "Are you sure?" I held the clipping up again for him to see.

This time he took it in hand and brought it close to his face. I had the impression that he was near-sighted.

"I don't mean to be rude," Sam said, "but how are your eyes?"

I could've kicked him for being so direct but Bromley actually smiled.

"That's a good question and I don't mind you asking. There's a lot wrong with me, but the one thing I got that's right—better than all right—is my sight." His gaze returned to the photo, but after several seconds of studying it, he shook his head again and returned the picture to me. "No, ma'am. I'm sorry but that definitely ain't him. That ain't the man that killed that lady and took to shooting at me. That just ain't him."

Sam said, "Look here, suppose we get the police over here with a sketch artist? They could—"

Bromley raised his hand. "No, sir. I don't want nothin' to do with no police."

My face must've shown my disappointment because Bromley apologized.

"I'm sorry," he said. "I won't talk to the police for you. But I can tell you what he looked like. Heck, I can even do you one better. I can show you."

"Show us? How?"

He pointed to one of the drawings he had tacked on the walls. It was the only one without joy in its face, the only one with death in its eyes.

CHAPTER 15

The portrait was of a man in his mid-thirties. A thick keloid scar roped down his face from the outer corner of his left eye to his throat. It was a detailed drawing, right down to the depiction of the intricate web of crows' feet around the man's eyes and a hint that his left eye was slightly smaller than his right. It was certainly as good as anything a police sketch artist would've come up with.

Bromley insisted upon giving it to us. We insisted on paying for it. We also tried our best to convince him to come with us. He wouldn't have to speak to the police unless he wanted to, we said. The newspaper would pay to put him up in a hotel where no one would find him. But his answer was always the same: a flat no.

"Don't worry about me," he said.

"Of course, I'm going to worry," I said.

"We're safe here."

"No. You're not."

"Do you have food?" Sam said. "And a gun?"

"I got both."

I didn't like it.

"Go on, you two," Bromley said. "I'll be fine. Just as long you don't tell nobody where you found me."

Sam and I hesitated, then gave him our word. Sam handed Bromley one of his calling cards. I took out one of mine and did the same. Bromley accepted the cards with a grateful smile, fingering them.

"If you need anything, or change your mind, then call us—either one of us," Sam said, then caught himself. Bromley obviously didn't have a phone. "I mean—"

"It's okay," Bromley said. "I ain't got no phone here, but I know where to find one, and I know how to use it." He slid the cards into his left shirt pocket, gave the pocket a little pat, then reached past us and unlocked the door.

I went out, feeling we'd made a terrible mistake. At the last minute, I turned and waved at him. That last image of him standing in the doorway would stay with me for years to come.

SAM and I agreed that Bromley's account rated a special edition and headed straight back to the newsroom that night. Sam went to this office to call the publisher to give him an update and then rang up the print room boys to tell them to come in.

Meanwhile, I hurried to my desk and started banging out a story. Typing rapidly, I described the stunning discovery of Slocum's body and his ties to Sharkey. I didn't mention any possibility of Vera having had an affair with Slocum. I didn't mention the notes and the indications of blackmail. And I didn't mention that a scarf thought to belong to her was found in Slocum's car. But I did note that it was believed that her body had entered the water close to where Slocum's car was found. The edition ran with the headline *Portrait of a Killer!* plastered across the top and the drawing prominently displayed beneath it. Next to it was a picture of Slocum. It hit the stands at midnight.

In the heat of the moment, putting out the special edition seemed like the wise thing to do. But within hours, I'd begun to wonder. If the gunman had had any doubts about Bromley's ability to identify him, that drawing must've dispelled them. I tried to tell myself that the gunman didn't know who Bromley was or where he lived, but then I'd think, *If Sam and I found him, then the killer could, too.*

When I returned to the newsroom the next day, my phone was ringing off the hook.

"You done dunnit again," one of the operators said. Her name was Gladys and she was in love with a married man who lived in Park Slope.

"You know what they say," I'd once told her, "that if he cheats on her, he'll cheat on you."

"Sure, he will," she'd said. "But guess what? I'm already cheating, too!" And then she'd given a raucous laugh.

Now, she sighed into the line. "You want me to stop putting calls through?"

"Nope, I've got to take them all."

"All right, fine. But next time, give a girl a bit of warning, won't cha?"

"Will do."

Most of the calls didn't amount to much. Most were to ask about a possible reward. The minute I said there wasn't one, at least not yet, the caller hung up. Others gave me their contact information and told me to call them back when there *was* a reward. After an hour and a half of taking calls and scribbling down notes, I was increasingly irritated. The calls so far had been useless.

My desk phone rang again and I simply stared at it. Should I answer? Or just give up?

I grabbed up the handset. "Lanie Price."

"Lanie."

That's all it took, him saying my name, for me to know who was calling and what mood he was in.

"Hello, detective."

"So you thought you'd pull a fast one over on me," Blackie said.

"Not at all."

"Get over here. Now. And bring it with you."

"Bring what?"

"And make sure it's the original," he said and hung up.

I'd barely put the receiver down when the phone rang again. This time the caller didn't even give me a chance to speak, not even to say my name.

"You say you were her friend. You sure don't act like it. You're supposed to protect her name, not smear it."

"I—"

"You linked her name to that—that *man.* You—"

"I wrote the facts, Levy. I simply wrote the facts."

"But why those facts? Why *those?*"

"Levy," I took a deep breath. "What we're trying to do is find the truth, and the only way—I repeat, the *only* way—to do that is to face facts, to not play fast and loose with them. Now, I don't know what Vera was doing in that car, but I—"

"Let me stop you right there. That's just it. You don't know for a fact that she was *even* in the car. You're making assumptions, and you're spreading them like lies. People will think—"

"We both know that Vera wouldn't have cared what

people 'think,' not in a situation like this. She would've wanted us to find her killer. That's what I'm helping the police to do."

"Are you? Or are you just trying to sell papers?"

He hung up before I could respond. I replaced the receiver, then rubbed my eyebrows, and took a moment. His reaction, though unpleasant, had not been entirely unexpected.

Somewhat like the coming conversation with Blackie would be.

I got up with a sigh and shouldered into my coat, then grabbed my bag and Bromley's drawing and headed out.

I was across the street, about to enter the police station, when I heard my name being called out.

"Miss Lanie!"

I turned to see Martin Del Ray hurrying toward me. He was gripping a copy of the special edition.

"This photo," he began, pointing to Slocum's picture.

"You recognize it?"

"This was the man I saw her with. *He's* the one. And now he's dead, too? Do you think she was killed because she was with him? That Levy found out and—"

"No," I raised a hand to quiet him. "I mean, there are plenty of theories, but we don't know anything yet. Nothing, for sure. But we will. And hopefully soon."

I opened the door to enter the station but he put an arm out, barring my way. "Find out soon. Find what you need and get him. Because if you don't, I will."

With that parting shot, he turned and stalked away.

FIFTEEN MINUTES LATER, I was sitting across from Blackie and handing over the drawing Bromley had made. Blackie gave it a glance, then set it aside, and eyed me with infinite irritation.

"This witness," he said, "you found him?"

"Yes."

"You're sure it's him?"

"Yes."

"When were you going to tell me?"

"But I did. I—"

"Never mind. Where is he?"

I swallowed. "I promised not to say."

"You *what?*" His nostrils flared. "Look here, Lanie, I've seen you do some crazy things and I've let you get away with them. But not this time."

I sighed inwardly.

"Tell me," Blackie insisted. "Tell me where this man is, what his name is and what he's told you. Do you understand? Because if you don't—"

"I know, I know. You'll put me in a jail cell faster than I can blink. "

"And don't think I won't. I—"

"Yes, yes, I know. The charge will be obstruction of a police investigation."

"Lanie—"

"I believe you. After all, you've done it before, haven't you? Thrown me in jail. But having done that, you know I won't—can't—give you what you want. He's a source—"

"He's a *witness*. That's what he is." He jabbed a finger at me. "I don't care what your so-called journalistic ethics tell you. He's a potential witness to a murder. You've got to turn him in."

"Turn him in? That's what you do with a suspect."

"Well, for all we know, he could've done it."

"How? He couldn't have been down below, fishing, and up there on that bridge, shooting them, at the same time."

"No, but he could've pretended to be fishing. He could've been lying in wait. That's what he could've been doing."

"Ridiculous," I said. "There's no way this guy could've been doing that."

"Oh, so I should take your word for it?"

"He's a good guy. If you only knew him—"

"Exactly. If I only knew him, could speak to him ..."

Enough of this.

"Instead of threatening me, you should be thanking me. For finding this witness—and for publishing the portrait." I tapped the drawing. "This is who you should be looking for."

Blackie shot me another look of exasperation, then gave up. He drew the portrait to him and studied it, his eyes narrowed. "It's very detailed. This witness, he's an artist?"

"A more than talented amateur."

Blackie gave a grunt. "Did this witness—can you at least give me a name?"

"No."

"All right, then," Blackie gritted his teeth. "Did he give you anything else, any further description of the guy?"

"Everything he remembered, he said, he put into that sketch."

Another grunt. He studied the drawing some more. "This is good," he admitted, finally. "But it's not enough." He straightened up and took out his pocket watch. "You've got two hours, two hours to get him back here, or I'll come looking for you."

It was time to do some accommodating or negotiating or to some degree both.

"Look," I said, "I can tell you one thing."

"And what's that?"

"I've connected Slocum to a loan shark."

"Yeah, Sam Sharkey," Blackie said. "What about it?"

I was as I'd suspected. Blackie had discovered the connection. On that, he was ahead of me. It was his new angle. "Well, I showed him Sharkey's picture. That's what."

Blackie's dark eyes narrowed. "Now, why'd you want to go and do that?"

"If you know about Sam Sharkey, then you already know why."

"Putting two and two together, were you?"

"Yeah, but in this case, I didn't come up with four."

"What does that mean?"

"It means he said Sharkey wasn't the shooter."

"No?" Blackie said.

"No." I shook my head.

"Hmph." Blackie rubbed his chin. "He was sure?"

"Absolutely."

"All the more reason I should talk to him."

"Well, what about you talking to Sharkey? My sources tell me he got out of jail two years ago. So, he's walking around, walking free."

"Now *that* he's most definitely not."

I inclined my head in a question.

"We hit Sharkey's townhouse last night," Blackie said.

Again, I should've known. "Find anything?"

He smiled darkly. "Wouldn't you like to know?"

"Oh, come on. I confirmed the existence of a witness, got you a portrait of the killer, and publicized it. And now I've given you pertinent information about what the witness saw. That's got to be worth something."

He pressed his lips together.

"Come on," I said. "Spill. You know you want to."

He held out for another thirty seconds. Then he started talking and didn't stop.

126

CHAPTER 16

"First of all, what exactly do you know about this loan shark?" Blackie asked.

I shrugged, playing dumb. "Just that he's a loan shark."

"Not just any loan shark," Blackie said, wagging a finger at me, "but the one-and-thank-God-only Sam Sharkey."

Sharkey, Blackie went on to tell me, was one of Harlem's most notorious moneylenders. At the height of his power, Sharkey charged as much as thirty percent in interest. "Not a month, mind you, but a *week*."

Sharkey could get away with it because people were desperate. Banks wouldn't lend to the colored and the poor. So, Sharkey used to say he was merely addressing a need. In fact, he was exploiting it. He claimed he was just taking advantage of an opportunity. In fact, he was simply taking advantage.

Physically, he was a little guy. "He's shorter than you, Lanie, but he's strong and as mean as a snake. He's suspected in the murders of at least three people and the torture of many others."

Sharkey's victims were mostly poor, small-time crooks,

drug addicts, or businessmen in default. Everyone else turned these kinds of people away, but Sharkey welcomed them, even solicited them. Because they were bad risks. He liked the fact that they couldn't pay. He knew it would put them at his mercy.

"Sharkey bought a townhouse in Bed-Stuy, out in Brooklyn, and had a sound-proof room built into the basement. He'd get people down there and torture them. One of those people was his own younger brother, Jimmy.

"Jimmy was one of his collectors. One day he took off with ten thousand dollars of his brother's money. Sharkey sent men after him. They found him in Atlanta and hauled him back. Sharkey had him chained to a radiator in the basement. Then he and two other men took turns beating him with an iron chain. His own brother. Sounds bad? It was. But all in all, Jimmy was one of the lucky ones. He survived."

I'd heard tell of what Sharkey had done to his brother, but as gossip. This was the first time I'd heard it confirmed.

Blackie went on. "This was about five, six years ago. The feds were on to him. They were talking to his people, watching every move he made. And Sharkey was feeling the heat. He was never the trusting type but now he turned paranoid. So, when he got word that the feds had gotten to one of his men, he took notice. It was idle gossip, but he believed it.

"The unlucky fellow name was Lonnie 'Lucky' Adler and he was a big guy. Weighed at least three hundred pounds. He worked as an enforcer, so he was no innocent, but a man with blood on his hands. Well, Sharkey had him brought down to that basement, and told him, 'I heard you been talking to the wrong people.'

"'Not true,' Adler said. 'I'd never do that to you.'

"The big man swore his loyalty up and down, swore it

on his mother's grave. It didn't matter. Sharkey had Adler strung up by a meat hook. Then he took a bat to him. Used it on Adler's hands and kneecaps. Adler begged and pleaded. He was loyal, he said. He'd never talk. It didn't matter. When the bat finally splintered, Sharkey reached for a hammer. Then an ice pick."

Blackie's words conjured gruesome images. Memories, really. Of crime scenes I wished I'd never visited, and of photos I wished I'd never seen.

The detective's voice rolled on. "Three days Adler took it. Three days. Then it was over. Sharkey had the big man's body tossed into a garbage dump.

"The feds knew Sharkey did it. Everybody knew. But folks were too scared to talk. So, the feds couldn't prove it. They couldn't prove murder. But what they *could* prove was tax evasion."

"Tax evasion?"

"Yup. Tax evasion."

Very original, I thought. We didn't know it at the time, but a few years later, the feds would use that same method to bring down Al Capone.

"It took them a while to build their case," Blackie said. "They finally did it by getting to the accountant."

"Slocum."

"Yup. Slocum. AKA Mason Lou Chiles. They got him to testify. I don't know how they did it, but they did. They managed to make him more scared of *them* than he was of Sharkey." Blackie's craggy face lit with a grim lopsided smile. "Now, *that's* saying something."

Blackie offered me a cup of java, his mood having greatly improved in the telling of his tale. He fetched me a cup, got one for himself, then said: "So, last night, while you were out talking to the witness, me and me boys, we were tossing Sharkey's place."

BLACKIE SANK down in a chair at Sharkey's parlor desk. He took a deep breath and let his gaze rove slowly around the room, touching on objects here and there, a figurine, photos, knickknacks and whatnot. Nothing but nothing he could use.

He blew out his cheeks, exasperated. There had to be something there. There was almost *always* something. And if he looked long enough, hard enough, he'd find it.

He rested his elbows on his knees. His feet slid forward and his toes hit the trashcan at the foot of the desk. He glanced down at it, saw nothing interesting, but decided to go through it anyway. Why not? He had nothing to lose.

He found the usual detritus: torn envelopes, receipts ...

Blackie paused, his fingertips touching the corner of a newspaper clipping. He pulled it out and felt a tingle of excitement. To his dawning delight, he saw that it was a photo of Slocum and Vera and Levy Kincaid, with a caption identifying each and mentioning Levy's church. The photo must've been taken at some church event.

Blackie was mulling over what he could do with this juicy tidbit when he heard a commotion at the door. He looked up to see that it was Sharkey himself, arguing with the officer guarding the entryway.

Blackie called out. "Let him in."

Sharkey stepped into the room, his chest puffed out and his mouth turned down. He was immediately belligerent. "What the hell are you guys doing in here?"

Blackie stood and explained, giving the news about the accountant's murder.

"Chiles? Dead?" Sharkey grinned. "Well, I'm glad somebody put his lights out. I won't deny it. But it wasn't me."

"You were angry at him. He testified against you."

"Aw, please," Sharkey waved it all away. "That trial happened a long time ago. I've moved on. Look, I got outta the slammer two years ago. If I was gonna put a hit on him, I wouldna waited two years to do it. Hell, I didn't even know he was here in New York. Last I'd heard, that piece of crap was in the wind."

"You knew," Blackie said. He held up the clipping.

"What's that?"

"Evidence. Proof that you knew about Chiles, knew his new name, and where he was working."

"I ain't never seen that before. Whatever it is, I ain't never seen it before."

"You had it in your trash."

"You put it in there."

"Oh, is that what you'll be claiming, is it? Well, we're going to check this and if we find your fingerprints on it, and we will, then—"

"All right, all right. It was in my trash. But I didn't have nothin' to do with that killing. I'm clean, I tell you. Clean."

"Sure, sure. Tell me another one. Now, turn around and put your wrists behind your back."

Sharkey shook his head, but complied, muttering oaths as Blackie snapped the handcuffs on him.

"Sam Sharkey, I'm taking you in the murders of Vera Kincaid and Mason Lou Chiles."

"Wait a minute. The who?" Sharkey twisted around, his eyebrows drawn together in a puzzled frown. "Who the heck is Vera Kincaid?"

"This clipping," Blackie told me now. "We think it's from a pamphlet. From Reverend Kincaid's church. There's a picture. Taken at a fundraiser. The photo shows the Kincaids and Slocum posing together."

"So, Sharkey saw the picture, recognized the man who helped put him away, and decided to put *him* away—for good."

"Looks like it. The fact that the witness says Sharkey didn't do it himself just goes to show that he hired someone else to do it."

"But why would Sharkey have put out a hit that included Vera?"

"I'm thinking wrong place at the wrong time. But trust me. We'll find out."

I should've felt relieved. Blackie had Sharkey in custody. But for how long? How long could he keep him? Sharkey's possession of a photograph clipped from a church pamphlet was circumstantial evidence at best.

"How about giving me ten minutes with him?" I asked.

Blackie grinned. "Dream on."

CHAPTER 17

I slept poorly that night and woke up feeling hung over. Tired and listless, I had a cup of coffee and a piece of buttered toast, then headed into the newsroom. I had just dumped my coat and purse on my desk when my phone rang. I grabbed it up and said, "Price."

A soft female voice spoke hesitantly. "Mrs. Price? Is this Mrs. Lanie Price?"

"Yes?" I sank down onto my office chair.

"I'm calling about the drawing, that picture your paper put out."

"Yes? What about it?"

"I think I know who it is," she said softly.

"Hmm-hmm." She wasn't the first person to have called and said she could identify the killer. "And who might that be?"

"My husband."

Let me amend that. She wasn't the first *woman* to have called and identified the man in the photo as that of a boyfriend or husband. So, I was prepared to be skeptical.

However, something about her tone of voice set her apart. I found myself reaching for a pen. "What's his name?"

A pause. And then, she wanted to meet, she said. "Do you have time to talk?"

There was fear in her voice. My stomach tightened. "When?"

"Now."

"Where?"

"Darleen's Fish 'n Fry. You know it?"

"The diner down on Lexington Avenue."

"That's the one. I'm a block away. I'll be in a booth near the front. Wearing a green hat. How long d'you need to get here?"

"Ten minutes."

"All right, but I can't wait no longer than that. Eleven and I'm gone."

TEN MINUTES. That's what I'd told her. Eleven and she said she'd leave. Ten. Eleven. I was there in twelve. A cabbie was dropping off passengers in front of the building when I left. I thought I was in luck. I jumped in and gave him the address. We were making good time, heading south on Lex, but then we hit a red light at 125th. I've never seen a light take so long. It didn't change, didn't change, didn't change. And when it finally did, there were people still crossing the road, moving slow, *slow*, *slooww*. And when they finally did move, the car in front of us didn't; it just sat like a big, black rock. The driver fiddling and fussing with his dashboard, then getting out to check under his hood, then standing there scratching his head. And me, telling my driver to pull out and go around and get going, *get going, GET GOING!* And him, telling me to stop telling him how drive.

Twelve minutes. Twelve lousy minutes by the time he pulled up in front of Darleen's. I shoved two bucks into his grubby hands, overpaying him by a mile, then hopped out and hurried inside, eyes scanning the place.

Darleen herself was standing behind the counter, wiping it down, and an old gent was sitting in the back, eating scrambled eggs and toast. Otherwise, the place was emptier than my refrigerator. There was no sign of a young woman in a hat, green or otherwise, not in the back or the front, the side or the center.

Not anywhere.

The diner had a bathroom in the back. I checked it, too. It was empty.

I hurried back to the front, leaned over the counter, and signaled Darleen. She sauntered over.

"What's the matter, baby? You look all bent out of shape."

"I'm supposed to meet someone here." I described her.

"Oh," Darleen said, raising an eyebrow. "Well, she didn't come in here. I would've seen her." She gestured to the front. "Take a seat. Maybe, she's late."

Late? She'd said she was only a block away. There was only one place with a public telephone. That was the drugstore. It was a block away, so she'd probably been calling from there. *One* block. What could've happened between there and here?

Maybe she'd tried to call me at the newsroom, while I was sitting in that cab, stuck in traffic.

Darleen set a cup of coffee down before me. "It's on the house."

I took a few sips, then let it grow cold. Five minutes

went by. Then ten. Then somehow it wasn't just fifteen. It was twenty. And she still wasn't there.

WELL, it certainly took me longer than twelve minutes to get back to the newsroom. I couldn't catch a taxi and ended up hoofing it. It was cold and windy, but I told myself that was good. There's nothing like the wind nipping at your tail to make you pick up your step. So I made it back in good time. I was actually feeling warm by the time I reached the building. But then the elevator didn't come, and I had to climb the stairs. So, by the time I got to the newsroom, I wasn't just warm but overheated, out of breath, and in one foul mood. I dropped down in my desk chair, not even bothering to take off my coat, and called the switchboard.

"Gladys, this is Lanie. You got any messages for me?"

"Nope. Not a one."

"No one called for me in say, the last hour?"

"Nope. Not a one."

"You're sure?"

"As sure as the shoe flies."

"As sure as the *what?*"

"The shoe flies. You know. The shoe? The shoe I threw at Oscar the other night?"

"You threw a shoe at Oscar?"

"Sure did. Got him smack upside the head. That'll teach him. The lousy cuss."

I had no idea she'd thrown a shoe at anyone, much less Oscar. My first instinct was to ask why. But I caught myself. If I asked that question, I'd be opening the gates to a conversation I didn't have time to have.

"Thanks," I said and put down the receiver.

I eased out of my coat. Did I have a bad feeling or did I have a bad feeling? That woman had seemed serious, like she'd thought long and hard before making a difficult decision. Had she changed her mind or had someone changed it for her? Her husband? Had he caught her? Had he been there or standing somewhere nearby when she made the call and then stopped her?

For a moment, I had a grisly image of a hand clamping around her mouth and dragging her back into the shadows.

"Lanie?"

I could just see it, two hands gripped her by the throat, closing tight, and squeezing.

"Hey, Lanie!"

I blinked and came to reality with a jerk. It was George Greene. He sat a couple of desks over from me and he was waving at me, trying to get my attention. He had two women sitting at his desk. They were identical, the only difference being the color of their outfits. One was in powder blue; the other in powder pink. For some reason, they looked familiar.

I nodded at him and Greene took it as permission to come over. I liked him, so that was fine.

"Those two, they're sisters," he said. "They came in right after you left. They say they want to talk to you and only you."

"About what?"

He frowned. "They won't say."

"All right. Send them over. Let me just borrow another chair."

"I'll fetch it," he said.

Once they were comfortably seated, Greene tapped his forehead in a goodbye salute and went back to his desk. I looked from one sister to the other. Up close, they looked even more familiar, but I still couldn't place them. I just hoped their business was simple -- maybe to invite me to a ladies' club charity event. Whatever it was, I hoped we could be done with it soon so I could go back to worrying about that woman. I glanced at the phone, hoping she'd call me back.

The twin in blue smiled. "I'm Ella Mae," she said. "And this here is Anna Mae." She gestured to the twin in pink.

Anna Mae gave a polite nod. It was the equivalent of a curtsy the way she did it. "We love your column," she said. "It's the main reason we buy this paper."

"Thank you." I flashed a brief smile. "So, what's this all about? How can I help you, ladies?"

"Well, actually ..." Ella Mae began. She glanced at Anna Mae, who encouraged her with a nod. Ella Mae continued. "We thought we might be helping you."

"Oh?" Admittedly, that piqued my curiosity.

"It's like this, miss. I work across the street, at the station house—"

"The *police* station?" Now, I was intrigued.

"Yes, ma'am. I'm one of the clerks."

Ah, I thought, realizing I must've seen her there.

"I know you in there a lot," Ella Mae went on. "They always talking about you."

I could well imagine who 'they' were and what they said. Not all the cops were happy with my friendship with Blackie. "Go on. You work at the station."

"Yes, and I ... Well, I ..."

"Go on," Anna Mae said.

"You see, we only supposed to look at the stuff we working on," Ella Mae said. "I mean, we *ain't* supposed to look at the stuff we not working on."

"I'm not sure I understand," I said.

"We know about the bruises," Anna Mae blurted out. "The bruises Mrs. Kincaid had. On her face."

"Oh," I said. "And you know about them how?"

"Like I said," Ella Mae swallowed. "We only supposed to look at the stuff we typing up. If we ain't working on it, then we not supposed to be looking at it."

"But you did. Correct?"

"Yes," Ella Mae said. "I mean, *I* did. Not Anna Mae. She don't work there. Just me. So, anyways, that's how I come to know about them bruises. They was in the medical examiner's report. And the day she got 'em, that was in the detective's report."

"OK," I said slowly. "So, you know about the bruises. What about them?"

The twins exchanged nervous glances. Ella Mae jerked a thumb at Anna Mae and said, "You tell it."

Anna Mae fidgeted. "Well, Ella Mae and me, we were talking about the case the other day. I mean, *everybody's* talking about it. And Ella Mae, she mentions them bruises, and how the reverend said he was out of town the day his wife got 'em, so he couldn't be blamed for them. So I say, 'What day was that?' And she tells me. And I say, 'Wait a minute.' And so, then I go to check, 'cause I remembered seeing something. And then I found it."

"Check what? Found what?"

"She works for the traffic court in Brooklyn," Ella Mae explained.

I still didn't get it.

"Maybe, I shouldn't say nothin'," Anna Mae said. "Maybe, it don't mean a thing."

"Maybe, it don't," Ella Mae said. "But maybe it do."

"I'm sorry," I said, "but *what* are you two talking about?"

"Well," Ella Mae said, looking at her sister. "Are you gonna tell her or should I?"

When Anna Mae hesitated, Ella Mae turned to me and opened her mouth, but before she could say a word, Anna Mae chimed in. "A traffic summons," they said in unison.

Ella Mae gave Anna Mae a look of annoyance. "Well, go on, then. Tell it."

"It had his name on it," Anna Mae said.

"Whose name?"

"The Reverend Kincaid's. He got a parking violation. Got it the very day she got them bruises. Got it and got served with a summons the next day. The officer who delivered it wrote down that he delivered the summons to the reverend personally."

Understanding dawned. "Oh, I see," I said softly.

I took down their contact information, thanked them, and promised Ella Mae I wouldn't tell Blackie that she'd been reading reports she wasn't supposed to. Then I sat back and thought about what they'd said. It might amount to something. It might also amount to nothing. But clearly, it meant I was going to have to have another difficult conversation with Levy.

But first ...

I glanced at the phone again, wondering. Perhaps, Gladys could confirm where the woman had called from. If it was the drugstore down the street from the diner, then I could—

My desk phone rang. Blackie again. He sounded uncharacteristically upbeat.

"Just calling to see if you've got any leads on the man in the drawing."

"Not really, no." I picked up a pencil and tapped my desk with it. "You're likely to find out before I do. Given the shooter's skills, he's probably been in trouble before and has a record. That's something you'd have access to, not me."

There was a pause, then a disappointed sigh. "It's all right, Lanie."

"What do you mean?"

"You can stop ducking and dodging."

"Excuse me?"

"I know about the soldier. And I know you know, too."

"That I—what?"

"We have the wife. Nabbed her maybe forty minutes ago. And we know she was on her way to see you."

"The wife?"

"Yeah, the wife."

"Oh, I see." Well, now at least I knew where she was—and that her husband hadn't done her in. I guess that was something. "How did you know she was on her way to see me?"

"We didn't. You just confirmed it."

My, my, my. He was having a good old time, wasn't he, yanking my chain.

He chuckled. "We picked her up just before she reached the diner. It was easy to put two and two together."

"How did you find out about her to begin with? Did someone drop a dime on her?"

"Let's just say we got a tip."

"You're holding her for questioning?"

"For now. We could make it for harboring a fugitive if she doesn't cooperate."

"He was at her house?"

"No. But he had been."

It would be a lousy thing to do, charge her with that, but I knew he was capable of doing it. "So, did you call me just to gloat?"

"I want you to talk to her, tell her what's good for her."

"And what would that be? That she'd better sing? That you'll keep her locked up if she doesn't?"

"That would be a good place to begin, yes."

"You can tell her that yourself."

"I already have."

I didn't respond.

"Look," he said. "You know me. I can go easy. Or I can go hard. I'm willing to go easy. For now. But my mood is changing fast."

I gazed out over the newsroom, over the heads of the other reporters bent over their Underwoods, to the dusty windows overlooking the street, and imagined Blackie at his desk, and a soldier's wife in holding.

"All right," I said. "I'll be right over."

CHAPTER 18

Letitia Glenn was like a lot of Harlem women her age: old before her time. She was probably in her late twenties but was already worn thin. She sat huddled on the cot in the jail cell, her coat drawn tightly around her. She was bitter toward me.

"I trusted you," she said. "You turned me in."

"Not quite." I informed her what Blackie had said.

She turned away.

"We don't have much time," I said. "I need you to talk to me. Right now."

"Why? So, you can go and tell *him?*" She gave a nod toward the world outside her bars, meaning Blackie.

"I won't tell him anything you don't want me to. I won't print anything you don't want me to. But *you* called me. You must've had a reason. Now's your chance. I don't know when you'll get another one. First things first: what's your name?"

"Letitia. Letitia Glenn. And my husband's name is Hiram." Tears slid down her cheeks. She sniffed and swiped them away with the back of her hand. More tears fell in rapid succession. "What am I going to do?" she whispered, her voice thick. "They want me to call him, get him to come in. They'll kill him if I do, but they gonna keep me locked up here if I don't. I can't stay here. I got a baby at home. And then there's them social workers. If they find out I'm here, they'll take my kid away. They just looking for a reason. They're vultures. All of 'em."

I took out a handkerchief and coaxed her into taking it. "Take a deep breath. And talk to me."

She mopped her face and balled up the handkerchief. "I wanted to tell you about Hiram, to explain. How he is. He's a good man, really."

How many times had I heard that one?

She must've sensed my skepticism because she rushed on. "During the war, he got hurt ..." She touched her forehead. "Up here. In his head. He wouldn't talk much about it, but one of his friends, he come by and told me what happened. They got caught in a minefield. Hiram didn't step on it, but he was close by when another guy did. The explosion, it sent him flying, and when he landed ... well, after that, he wasn't the same no more. They sent him home."

All right. I'll admit. That did soften me up. A little.

She drew her knees up and hugged them. "We was so happy to see him. He looked fine. Didn't look like nothing was wrong with him. But then it started. The headaches, the forgetting things. He couldn't remember nothing, and he'd wake up screaming and sweating in the middle of the night."

By now, I was thinking of what she must've been going through, living with a man like that, as much I was thinking of him.

She rocked a little, back and forth, back and forth. "One day, he just went plum crazy. He was working in the grocery store down the street. Locked himself back in the stock room, wouldn't come out. They had to come and get me. Course I lost money that afternoon, cause I had to leave work early and the boss said he wasn't gonna pay me for the time I wasn't there. We needed the money, but Hiram needed me more. It's just that, well, it wasn't the first time and it wasn't gonna be the last. It took me an hour to talk him out of there."

She had me. I admit it. She had me.

"They had him in that hospital for a while. Bellevue. I used to visit him there. He'd be sitting there, holding his head. Said he could hear this kinda hum, like somebody was chanting. And then he'd start pulling at his clothes, saying they was too hot for him, that he was burning up, and then it was just like he was seeing things. Like he didn't see me, didn't know where he was—no, it was like he was back there. I don't know what they put our men through over there, but it show 'nough ruined them. Not all of them. But I'm telling you, even the ones that look like they sane, they got a little crazy in 'em. If they was over there, they got a little crazy. They just done learned to bury it, to hide it, but they got it."

She lowered her legs, let them hang over the edge of the mattress and looked downward. "Hiram told me he wanted to die. Said it would've been better if he hadn't come back. Leastways, me and the baby, we would've gotten a little bit of money out of it. I told him that weren't true. That he was what I wanted, what me and the baby needed. But it didn't matter. He couldn't hold on. You know what I mean? He just couldn't hold on.

"And the people, they didn't understand. Or care. They looked at him and they didn't see no hero. He was just one more shiftless Negro. That's all he was to them."

For the first time since I'd come in, she gazed directly at

me. "It did something to him, ma'am. I swear it did. He had swagger when he come back. He had pride. But the nightmares, the shakes, they took it all away from him. But it was the people here, and how they looked at him, that's what really brought him down. And it didn't matter none what I said or did. It really didn't matter. 'I'm broke,' he said. 'Lettie,' I'm broke and you can't fix me.' Then he walked on out."

"When was that?"

"'Bout five years ago."

"But you've seen him since then?"

"Not that much. I know he went to work for a man named Sharkey. I'm guessing he didn't want to do it, but he couldn't find nothing else, so he went back to doing what he knew how to do: fighting and killing. Only this time it weren't for no Uncle Sam."

"How'd you find out what he was doing?"

"People, gossiping, running their mouths. I told them to hush up, that he was doing the best he could. But deep down, I ached for him. He deserved better than that."

"So, when was the last time you saw him?" I asked, thinking of Blackie's threat to charge her with harboring a fugitive.

"It had been a while. I was beginning to think maybe he was dead. Then he showed up day before yesterday. Told me he needed a place to stay till he got back on his feet. Gave me a hundred dollars. I gotta be honest. I knew something was wrong. I wondered what he'd been up to."

"Did you ask him? "

"No ... no, I didn't." She looked down and an expression of shame flitted across her face. "I guess I just didn't want to know."

"I understand."

"We got a baby girl, you see. Annabelle. She six now.

And oh, how she loves her daddy. So when he came, she was so happy to see him, you know? So, happy. He's always been good to her, good to me. Always been gentle with us. And we, we really needed the money."

She told me how she'd come home the day before to find Hiram there. "That's his way, you know? I never know when he's going to show up. I just know that he will. Eventually."

He was sitting on the living room sofa, with Annabelle snuggled up beside him. "He bought her a little doll. Funny. It looks just like her. Cute and ... well, a pretty little thing. And he got her a book. He was reading it to her when I walked in."

"MAMA! MAMA!" Annabelle jumped up from the floor and ran to her mother. She held up the doll. "Look what daddy got me, Mama! Look!"

Letitia bent and caught the bundle of energy flying her way and gave her a hug. She smiled at the doll and looked over at her husband. Her breath caught at the sight of him, partly because she still loved him so, partly because she ached to see how life was aging him before his time.

"Hiram," she said.

"I–I just stopped by right quick to say hello. I don't mean to cause no trouble."

"Can daddy stay for supper?" Annabelle asked.

Hiram said, "No, baby, I can't. I—"

"Oh, please, Daddy, please!" Annabelle cried.

Hiram hesitated. "Well, if your mama says—"

"Mama, you'll say yes, right? Daddy can stay. He can eat with us, right?"

Letitia looked into her baby's earnest brown eyes and

knew she couldn't deny her. "All right. Fine. He can stay. For dinner."

"And he can put me to bed, too, right, Mama? He can put me to bed?"

Letitia's gaze shifted to meet Hiram's.

"I'd love to do that, Lettie. If you'll let me."

Annabelle's threw her chubby arms around Letitia's neck and whispered. "Please, Mama."

"OK," Letitia said softly. "OK."

"I KNOW you gonna think I'm crazy for saying this, but Hiram ... he's a good man," Letitia now told me. "Always been a good father. When he was home, he was home. He was never out there, doing what a lot of men do, gambling and drinking and carrying on. He was home with us, or working—or looking for work. When he's there, he's *really there.* You know what I mean?"

I nodded, trying to keep my expression neutral.

I thought I'd succeeded, but she must've seen something, perhaps something that reflected her own thoughts, because she gave a bitter little smile and chuckled. "Yeah, I know what you're thinking: Problem is ... he's just not there that often."

"Letitia," I said, "I'm not here to criticize."

"No?" She raised an eyebrow.

"No."

"Just to accuse, then." She held my gaze. "Your paper. The police. Y'all think he killed that preacher's wife. I don't know if he did or didn't. But I'm scared for him. They gonna hunt him down, like an animal. I know it. I seen it before." She looked away, haunted by images she obviously didn't want to see. "Back down there in Georgia, where I

148

come from, I seen it before. And I … well, I don't want him to go like that."

She unfolded the handkerchief and spread it on her lap with shaking fingers. "After I saw his picture in your paper, I sat for a while, just thinking. And it came to me that maybe, just maybe, if I got him to you first, then you could write about him, get his story. And then maybe …" She gazed at me, her lips trembling lips. "But that was a fool's dream, wasn't it? You writing about him, getting sympathy for him, sympathy and understanding?"

I shook my head, not liking what I was about to say, but thinking it best to say it, anyway.

"The police," I began, "are a power unto themselves. You and I, we both *know* that. And chances are that no amount of coverage by some little colored paper is going to change how they treated your man. But," I paused, "that doesn't mean we can't try."

That, at least, got a smile out of her.

"However," I went on, "there's something else you've got to remember."

She listened intently.

"Your husband," I said, "is suspected of having killed a very well loved member of the Harlem community. You're worried about the white folk? What you should be worried about is the colored ones."

She nodded mutely. I didn't like talking to her like that, but I didn't see a reason to lie. What I could've added, but didn't, was that she was talking to a friend of the victim. That's not to say I didn't feel for her and her man. After listening to her, I surely did. But I felt for my friend, too.

Again, she must've sensed something, seen something in my face.

"I know I'm asking a lot of you," she said. "That lady, that woman y'all say he killed, she was one of your kind.

Maybe you even knew her. Don't think I don't know that. But please remember this: my husband didn't start out this way. He went to war, risked his life for this country, and it kicked him to the curb when he got back. Ain't nobody reached out a hand to help him."

All true. But it was also true that there were a lot of men that had happened to. And not all of them turned into killers.

"I'll tell his story fair and square," I said.

"I guess I can't ask for more than that."

"About the police. What are you going to do?"

"They'll kill him if I call him and get him to come in." She bit her lower lip, her forehead puckered. "What would you do?"

I gave her a reassuring smile. "I think you already know what you need to do."

She thought a little more, then gave a small nod. "Tell that detective I'm ready."

CHAPTER 19

T en minutes later, we were both sitting at Blackie's desk.

"So, you know where he is?" Blackie asked her.

"No." Letitia shook her head. "But I know where to call and leave a message. Then we got to wait till he calls back."

Blackie glanced at me.

I gave a little shrug. "Makes sense to me."

He looked annoyed but gave in. "Who'll you call?" He put his hand on the phone.

"It's a pool hall over on 130th Street. He likes to go over there sometimes. Gets messages there."

"Would he hide out there?"

"Don't think so. There ain't no room for nobody to hide over there. Besides, the owner, he says he'll only take messages and Hiram said he had to pay him to do that."

Blackie still looked skeptical, but he pushed his phone over to her. "Make the call." He handed her a slip of paper. "And leave this number."

"What's so special about that one?" I asked.

"The switchboard knows to put the call through

without identifying the station house or asking the caller who he wants to speak to."

"Oh, so he won't know he's calling the cops."

"Exactly."

Letitia glanced at me. I nodded for her to go ahead. She picked up the note with trembling fingers and gave the operator a phone number. The call went through. She asked for a "Mr. Belcher," and when he came on the line, she left the phone number, speaking in soft voice. Then, she hung up and turned to Blackie. "Can I go now?"

Blackie gestured to the officer standing at the door. "Take her back to the cell."

Letitia's eyes widened. "But I thought you said you'd let me go."

"I asked you to talk to him. You haven't done that yet."

"But the baby sitter. She's gonna leave soon."

"I'm sorry, but no." Blackie shook his head.

Letitia looked at me, stricken.

"Blackie, can you at least let her go home to check on the babysitter?" I asked.

He raised an eyebrow. "If I let her go, do you honestly think she'd come back?"

"I would. I would. I promise I would," Letitia said.

"Maybe, you would," he said, "but no. You have to be here when he calls back. And since we don't know when that'll be, you have to stay."

"Well, at least give her a phone call," I said. "Let her call home and talk to the babysitter."

"Please," Letitia begged.

He thought about it. "All right, fine."

Letitia's fingers shook as they dialed the number, but she managed to make her voice sound firm. There was a brief conversation with the babysitter, a "Mrs. Ledge," and then her voice changed. It softened, became reassuring.

"Baby, Mama's got to work tonight, OK? So, I'll be home tomorrow. You be a good girl, you hear? Listen to Mrs. Ledge. Do what she tell you to. And let her brush your teeth, baby. Let her brush your teeth. … Yes, I promise. I'll be home tomorrow."

I stared at Blackie hard, not bothering to hide what I thought of him. "I understand the need to catch this guy. Believe me I do, but this is not the way to go about it."

"Oh, you have a better way? Tell me about it."

Letitia finished her call and put the receiver back in its cradle. She took a deep breath and set her shoulders. Blackie nodded at the officer. He reached out to take her by the elbow. She drew back, swept past him and set off back down the hallway, her head held high, her steps resolute.

"She's got guts," Blackie said, watching her go.

"Yeah, and integrity, too," I said, looking at him.

He tightened his jaw, making the muscles bulge. "Well, I guess, you can leave."

"Since I'm here, I'd like to talk to Sharkey."

"He's not receiving visitors."

"I'm not a visitor."

Blackie regarded me with ill-disguised annoyance. "No."

"Later?"

"Not likely."

"Well, will you at least tell me what he's said?"

Blackie shrugged. "There isn't all that much to tell."

EARLIER THAT DAY, before I got there, Blackie had indeed had several words with the loan shark. He'd had him brought into one of the interrogation rooms, sat him down under the lights, and started the questioning.

"We know your history with Chiles. You had motive. You had means. And when you found out where he was, you sent someone to kill him."

"Oh, come on. If you're talking about that clipping, you got nothing. You say it's him that was in that picture. I guess I gotta believe you. Cause I sure didn't recognize him. That picture don't look nothing like the way I remember him."

"It's close enough. Remember, we have photos of him from the days of the trial. Sure, he might've put on a pound or two, gotten a little grayer around the gills, but it's him."

"I tell you, I—"

Blackie pounded the table. "Stop lying! Now, who sent you the clipping?"

"I don't know, I tell ya! I don't know! I got it in the mail. I thought it was junk and threw it away. That's why you found it where you found it. In the garbage."

Blackie straightened up. He tossed a folder down on the table, opened it. It was a copy of the drawing, cut from the special edition of the *Harlem Age*. Blackie shoved the picture under Sharkey's nose, tapped it.

Sharkey glanced at it, then shrugged and looked away. "I don't know him."

"Yeah. You do." Blackie walked slowly around the table. "Army vet by the name of Hiram Glenn. We know he's muscle for you." Blackie leaned down, put his fists on the table, and said, "And we know he pulled the trigger on Chiles."

"All right, all right. He worked for me. So, what? He don't no more. He was too crazy, even for me. And if he did do Chiles, then that's on him. I didn't have nothing to do with it. Nothing, I tell you. I ain't had nothing to do with it."

"So, he's admitting to knowing Glenn," Blackie told me.

"But denying everything else."

"He can deny all he wants. We know he did it."

"And he knows you don't have any proof."

CHAPTER 20

I headed home after leaving the police station. But when I hit my block, I found myself walking past my door, down to the Kincaid house. Levy answered my knock within minutes. I'd wondered if he'd even talk to me, given his reaction to my article, but ever the gentleman, he waved me in, instructed Beulah to bring us some coffee, and led me into the parlor.

"I want to apologize," he began, "for the way I spoke to you earlier."

"That's OK."

"No. It's not. You're trying to help. And you're right. Vera would've wanted the truth to come out. She was a brave woman, and I firmly believe she never would've done something to be ashamed of. She deserves to have the truth come out, come what may."

His face was drawn. His eyes were bleary. The man was obviously getting very little sleep. He ran a hand across the top of his sleek head, gave an exhausted sigh, and sank down on his parlor sofa. I eased down in the armchair opposite him.

"So," he said, "what brought you here this fine evening? Tell me you've brought some good news. 'Cause I sure could use some."

I hesitated, not sure where to begin, *how* to begin.

"Come on." He gave me an encouraging smile. "Come out with it."

"I—"

Beulah entered with the coffee tray. Conversation waited while she served us. Levy called after her as she started out. "Would you mind closing the doors?"

"Of course, Reverend." She backed out and drew the parlor pocket doors together behind her.

"So," he said to me. "Continue."

"Well," I said, "I have it on good authority that you were here in town the day Vera got those bruises."

Surprise flashed in his eyes, followed hard by a spark of fear that was quickly repressed. "Your sources—that's what you people call them, right? They must be mistaken. I—"

"You were here in town. There's use denying it. They have proof."

He was quiet a moment, thinking. "This proof. Have you seen it?"

"Not yet."

"Then how can you be so sure—"

"Levy, these are the kind of people who, if they say they have proof, have proof. Now tell me why you were here that day."

He shrugged. "It was nothing, really."

"What do you mean 'nothing?'"

He didn't answer.

"Levy, please. Talk to me. Why did you lie to the police, to *me?*"

"But I didn't. Not ... totally."

I waited.

He wiped his face with his hands. "I really was out of town for those couple of days. I was in Philadelphia for a case. Then I came back to get a file."

"A *file?*"

"I needed it for my appointment with our accounting firm. After I fired Slocum, I asked our tax accountants to take a look at our books. But I forgot one of the files I needed. I was sure I'd packed it but somehow, in all my haste, I forgot it. So that day, the day you're talking about, I drove back, went to the church office, and grabbed it. Then I got something to eat and checked into a hotel."

"Why didn't you go home?"

"I don't know." He shrugged. "It was late. And I had to get up early the next day to start back. I didn't want to disturb Vera. I didn't want to have to explain, you know? I just wanted to go to bed. Get some sleep. So I stayed at a hotel. Easy. Uncomplicated."

"As in ... talking to Vera had become complicated?"

"I didn't say that."

"You suggested it."

"Now, wait just a minute." He rose to his feet.

"You lied to me," I said, also rising up. "You lied, Levy. Lied to my face, lied to the police."

He started to protest, then pressed his lips together and took a moment. "Look, I'm sorry. Sorry I wasn't upfront with you." He licked his lips and swallowed hard. "But when it comes to the police, I ..." His jaw tightened and his nostrils flared. "Hm-hmph. No way."

I understood his skepticism toward the police. Of course, I did. But I needed him to understand that he was making himself look suspicious. And that sometimes, you had to have faith.

"You know, Levy, most of the time, the police don't pay all that much attention to murders in Harlem, not when it involves a colored man, much less a colored woman. But they're paying attention to this one. From where I'm standing, they're actually making a good-faith effort."

"Are they?"

"Yes, they are. They're doing everything they can to find your wife's killer and you should be helping them. Instead, you're standing in their way."

His jaw moved. "Lanie, do you really trust this cop?"

"I do."

"Why?"

"Because I've seen his work."

"I see. So he's the exception. 'Cause you know the general wisdom out here is that we can't—our kind—we can't trust a cop, can't afford it. 'Cause they're not here to protect us. Not us. They're here to *arrest* us, pure and simple."

"I know. Trust me, I know—"

"Do you? Do you really understand?"

"What I *understand* is this: Your wife's dead. She's been taken from you in a brutal, horrible way. But all you're thinking about is protecting your back."

"That's not fair."

"No, maybe, it's not. But it's where we are."

"Vera would want me to—"

"What she'd want you to do is tell the truth. She'd want you to help them find the person who gunned her down."

"That's exactly what I'm doing."

"By lying?"

"By keeping them on the straight and narrow. Yes, if you want to know, to keep them from looking at me. From *wasting time* by looking at me. 'Cause I sure as shooting know I didn't kill my wife, and I hope you know it, too. So, every minute, every second they spend looking down the loupe at me, that's another minute, another second they could be spending on finding the man who did this. You know what keeps me awake at night? What makes me break out in cold sweats? It's the thought that they won't get it right. That they'll take the easy way out—"

"The easy way being to blame you?"

"Yes. If I give them half a chance, they'll twist my words, use them against me. You want them to do that to me, to do that to Vera? Have them lock me up and let the real killer go free?"

I took up my purse and gloves. He was tired. And confused. And I was suddenly feeling that way, too. "I'll talk to you later," I said and started out, but his voice caught me at the door.

"I'm sorry, Lanie," he said, standing behind me. "You didn't deserve that."

I turned back to him but said nothing.

"I–I'm just–I don't know what to do," he said. "Somebody out there—*Somebody out there*"—and here he jabbed at the world outside his door—"killed my wife. Took her. *Destroyed* her. But instead of looking for whoever did that, they're just looking for a reason to come here—*here to her home, our home*—and accuse me of having done it."

"Levy, they're not—"

"Yes, they are. They don't understand, but you should. I loved her. I never laid a hand on her. I would've laid down my life for her."

My irritation faded in the face of his anguish. "I know, Levy. I know," I said wearily, gently. "Don't worry. The truth will come out. I promise you, the truth will come out. As a matter-of-fact, maybe I shouldn't tell you this, but they've already taken someone in for questioning."

His mouth dropped open in slack-jawed relief. "They got the man?"

"They've got ... someone. He may not be the one who actually pulled the trigger, but they think he knows who did."

"Why didn't you tell me?" he whispered. "Why didn't you say something?"

"Because they don't have proof, Levy. They don't have anything real. Nothing that'll stand up in court."

"You mean, they might have to let him go?"

"I don't know."

"But they think they've got the right person?"

"They're sure they do."

He thought about that. "Who is it?"

"Nobody you'd know."

"But—"

I held up a hand. "The point," I said, "is that you don't need to worry about them looking at you, not anymore. What you do need to think about is getting your story straight and keeping it that way. Now, tell me," I said, stepping up to him, "what hotel did you stay at?"

CHAPTER 21

Early the next day, I went straight to the police station. Blackie assured me that Hiram Glenn had not shown up at the pool hall or called back.

"You think he got the message?" I asked.

"I sure hope so," he said. "She swears that the guy's always been dependable in giving it to him."

"You've got people watching the place?"

"Two cars. If he shows up, they'll get him."

I asked about Letitia. "Can I see her?"

"Sure."

Letitia sat up when she saw me, stood stiffly, and came to grip the bars. She had double bags under her eyes. "My kids?"

"They're fine," I said. "I called yesterday evening and then I called again this morning. She said your babies slept well."

"You told her I'm down here, arrested?"

"I told her ... you were indisposed."

"Indisposed," she repeated slowly. She gave a grim little smile. "Thanks for saying that. It seems so ... so ladylike."

The smile melted into an expression of despair. She glanced up at the guard. "They not going to let me out of here, are they? Not till they get him."

I thought about that, then chose to answer the best way I knew how. "Don't think like that. Have faith."

There was a jangling of keys behind me. It was an officer. He let Letitia out, escorted her to Blackie's office and gestured for her to take a seat at a small table they'd set up with a phone. They had another phone set up on a nearby table.

It was good timing. Lettie had barely sat down when the telephone rang. Blackie held up a finger, indicating she should wait, then strode over to the second phone. He picked up the receiver, but held the cradle down, then gave her a nod.

Lettie picked up the phone. "Hiram?" she said, her hand at her throat.

Blackie released the cradle and put his hand over the mouthpiece, so he could listen in. I hurried over to stand next to him. He gave me a look of annoyance but held the phone so we could both listen.

"Is that you, baby? Really you?" Hiram was saying.

"Yes, it's me. It's really me. How are you?"

"What you'd expect?"

"Honey, they got your picture in the paper. If you come—"

"They not gonna let me come in, baby. They never gonna let me face trial. If they don't shoot me on the doorstep, they'll beat me to death, say I was resisting. Or hang me in my cell. Say I did to myself."

"Hiram—"

"You were right to make me leave, Lettie. I messed up bad this time. I need to stay away. That's the only way I can protect you."

Letitia hesitated, then glanced up at me, pleadingly. *What can I say? What* should *I say?*

"Lettie?" Hiram said. "You still there?"

"Yes, yes. I'm still here. I—"

"The police is listening, right? They making you make this call, right?"

"Hiram, I—"

"Don't worry about it, baby," Hiram said gently. Then his tone hardened. "Mr. Policeman. I know you listening. Well, I'm telling you. I'm not coming in. I'm not making it easy for you."

Blackie dropped all pretense. "You should really take another think, fella. Turn yourself in."

"Why? So you can kill me? We both know how that works."

"You listen to me, you scalawag, I've got your wife here. Yes, here, in the station. She's got very fine accommodations back in our jail cell. Right now, it's temporary. But I can make it permanent."

"You can't do that—"

"Oh, I can and I will. I know you were at her house. She fed you, gave you a place to rest, maybe even sleep. That's called harboring. I'll file the charge and make it stick. If you don't want that to happen, then you'd better do the manly thing and turn yourself in."

Silence followed.

Then Hiram said, "All right. But first, I've got some business to take care of. I'll be in touch." Before Blackie could say more, there was a click. Hiram had hung up.

Blackie slammed down the receiver. He turned, pointed at Letitia, and told the uniform on guard, "Book her."

I stared at him hard, not bothering to hide what I thought of him. "I understand the need to catch this guy. Believe me I do, but this is not the way to do it."

"Oh, you have a better way? Tell me about it."

We had a staring contest. Usually, it was Blackie who gave in, but this time, it was me.

"I'll write about this," I said. "I'll—"

"Good. Write about it. Make sure he knows about it. Make sure he knows I mean business. That I—"

His phone rang, cutting him off. A look of harried resentment flashed across his face. He snatched up the handset and identified himself with a brusque, "Detective Blackie." He listened. His brow furrowed. He rubbed the space between his eyes and his gaze shifted to me. "All right." He hung up and turned to me. "That was for you."

"Me? Then why didn't you—?"

"It was the desk sergeant. Sam left a message. Said he just got a call from a man named Bromley."

Bromley? If he'd taken the chance of leaving his cabin, had gone to the trouble of finding a phone to call us, then he was in trouble. "What did he say?"

"That Bromley's changed his mind. That he, Sam, is already on his way to see him and that you'd better get out there. Fast." Blackie eyed me. "This Bromley, he's the witness, isn't he?"

I stood. "I've got to go."

"Not without me, you don't." He grabbed his hat and coat and shot me a glance that dared me to object.

I wasn't about to. If anything, I was actually glad Blackie was coming along. Something had happened to make Bromley fully realize the danger he was in. This was the chance to get him the protection he needed. I just hoped it wasn't too late.

CHAPTER 22

S am was already at Bromley's shack by the time we got there. I introduced Blackie to Bromley. Bromley didn't like Blackie's being there—you could see it in his eyes—but he gave in with a nod, stepped back, and let us in.

The killer had been there, Bromley said.

"Did he hurt you or Ruthie Anne?" I asked.

"We weren't here. I'd done took Ruthie Anne over to a neighbor's house so she could see her friends. Then I come back here and found this."

"I thought you said you weren't going out."

"I know, but me and Ruthie Ann, we was going crazy, staying in here. After you two left, it got worse. It was like being in stir. We just had to get out, get some air."

"Well, lucky you did," Sam said, looking around.

The place had been trashed, Bromley's meager possessions had been destroyed, the pictures and shelves ripped from the walls, the legs of the table knocked out from under it.

"Nothing's gone," Bromley said. "It's all here, just

broken, in pieces. Then there's this." He pulled back the curtain that hid the cot. The intruder had used Bromley's chalks to scrawl a message in large crude letters over the bed.

KEEP YOUR MOUTH SHUT!

"You two can't stay here," I said.

This time, he agreed.

Blackie interviewed Bromley on the spot, confirming what I'd told him but getting nothing more. Then he offered to take Bromley in protective custody. Bromley refused.

Sam said, "Why don't you and Ruthie Anne stay in a hotel instead."

"I ... I—"

"The paper will foot the bill," Sam said.

Bromley was surprised. To be honest, so was I. Footing a hotel bill isn't cheap and our publisher had a tendency to watch every cent.

"Why would you do that?" Bromley asked.

"It's a good idea," Blackie said. "Mr. Bromley, we've got a dangerous man out there and he's coming for you. So, instead of chasing after him, we set a trap—"

"And use me as bait?" Bromley said.

"No!" I objected. "You wouldn't."

"It makes the most sense," Sam said. "It would be the fastest way of catching this guy."

"But you'd be putting his life in danger," I said.

"We can offer protection," Blackie said.

"I can't believe you two would even—"

"Excuse me—" Bromley said.

"Suggest something like that," I went on. "You'd be risking the life of our one and only witness."

"I'm telling you, we can protect—"

"*Excuse me—*" Bromley tried again.

"And what about Ruthie Anne? And the danger you'd be putting her in? When I think of all the things that could go wrong—"

"*EXCUSE ME!*" Bromley yelled.

We all jumped. Bromley looked from me to Blackie to Sam.

"Would y'all please stop talking 'bout me like I'm not here," he said. "I *am* here, and I got a say in what goes on."

"Of course, you do, but—" I began.

"Nah, Miss Lanie. There ain't no ifs, ands, or buts about it. This is *my* life and I gets to say what I'm gonna do with it. Now, the detective here, if he says the fastest way to get this all over with is to use me as bait, then I'm all for it. Now, Mr. Detective, you say you can protect us?"

"Yes," Blackie nodded. "I can."

"What about ... what about Ruthie Annie?" I asked.

There was a pause, a moment of silence.

"She can come stay with me," I said. "I have a house. She can have a room all to herself. She can stay with me, till this is all over."

Bromley thought about it, nodded. "OK. That sounds good."

"We'd better go get her now," Blackie said.

But when we went over to Bromley's neighbor and explained to Ruthie Annie that she was to stay with me a while, she threw her small arms around her grandfather's neck and refused to leave him.

Bromley tried to tell her it would only be for a little while, but she wouldn't hear of it. She tightened her hold on him and buried her face in the crook of his neck. He looked over at us apologetically. "I guess she been through too much loss already. First her papa, then her mama. She too scared of losing me to let me go."

I nodded. "I understand." I reached over and stroked

her hand. "We're going to do our best, Ruthie Anne." I threw a glance at Blackie and Sam, who stood next to one another. "Our *very* best to make sure nothing happens to you and your grandpa, you hear?"

She nodded and bent her head against to rest it on Bromley's shoulder.

I went over to Blackie. "Well, detective, you've got your work cut out for you. Let's see what you can do."

WE INSTALLED Bromley and Ruthie Anne in a small hotel over on 145th Street and Broadway. Sam said he had to head back to the newsroom. "Lanie, you coming?"

"In a minute. I'll be right behind you."

"Should I wait for you?"

"No, you just go ahead. I'll be right there."

Sam slightly canted his head to one side. His gaze flitted from me to Bromley to Blackie.

"Don't worry," Blackie said. "I won't let her stay."

"I don't intend to," I said.

"All right," Sam said. "Then, I guess I'll see you back at the office."

"I don't think I'll be back in tonight, Sam, but tomorrow morning."

"Fine." Sam opened the door and stepped out.

Blackie turned to me. "You heard what I told him."

"Like I said. I don't intend to stay." I turned to Bromley and gestured toward Ruthie Anne. "Last chance, Ruthie Anne. Now that you've seen where we have your grandpa stashed, maybe you feel better?"

Vaguely, I heard the sound of distant voices raised.

"You can still come with me, if you want."

Out in the corridor, the noise level increased. Someone shouted. There was the sound of running feet.

Ruthie Anne looked to Bromley. "Grandpa?"

He bent down, took her by the hand. "Baby, it's gonna be OK. You can go with the nice lady. I'm gonna be fine."

More voices. More shouts. And now a siren screamed in the distance. Blackie and I exchanged glances.

"What in the blue blazes ..." Blackie unholstered his gun, hurried to the door and cracked it open. A thin smell of smoke wafted in. Groups of hotel guests, many still in night robes, were hurrying past.

"What's going on?" Blackie asked.

Everyone ignored him. Blackie stuck his head out, looked left and right, then came back inside, shutting the door behind him.

"I smell smoke," Bromley said.

"Is there a fire?" I asked.

Blackie holstered his gun. "I'm going to go downstairs and see what's going on. You guys stay here. Lock the door after me and don't open it to anybody but me."

"But—"

He was out before Bromley could finish his sentence. Bromley started for the door, but I got to it first and locked it.

Bromley objected. "Look, I know smoke when I smell it. If this place is on fire, it'll go up like a wood pile. We gotta get outta here."

"Let Blackie find out what's going on."

"But it's clear what's—"

"No, It could be the killer."

"But he doesn't know where we are."

"How do you know? Are you sure? I'm not. We can't risk going out there."

"And I won't risk staying in here. I'm not about to let me and my grandbaby cook to death."

"Please," I said. "Give Blackie at least another five minutes."

The sound of the siren grew closer. At the same time, the sounds outside the door began to recede.

Another minute passed. The smell of smoke grew thicker.

"Come on, baby," Bromley said, reaching for Ruthie Anne. "We're leaving. Everybody's out but us. We got to go." He grabbed her hand.

I stood in front of the door. "The gunman, he could be waiting outside the door."

"I'm leaving," Bromley said, "and there ain't nothing you can do to stop me."

I looked from him to the child. She was terrified, clutching her doll, but she was silent, mature enough not to panic or cry.

"That detective," Bromley said. "He should've been back by now. The fact that he—"

"All right," I said. "We'll go. But hurry and keep your faces covered." I unlocked the door, peeped out, then held it open and stood aside.

The corridors were empty, eerily so. Perhaps, there were a few like us who had tried to hold out in their rooms but most were gone. The place felt abandoned.

"Hurry," I told them and pointed down the corridor. The three of us ran as fast as we could, coat collars held over our noses. We pushed open a swing door with a glass panel in it, to enter another corridor. Then ran pell-mell down another corridor. Suddenly, the place seemed endless. Where was the exit door?

Bromley was in front, Ruthie Anne in the middle, holding on to his hand, and I brought up the rear, constantly looking over my shoulder, hoping to see Blackie, fearing to see Hiram Glenn. Suddenly, I thought I saw a shadow, darker than the smoke, looming up behind me.

"Go! Go!" I cried. "Hurry!"

That's when it happened.

Ruthie Anne stumbled and fell. The doll flopped out of her hand. Bromley hauled the child to her feet and dragged her forward, but she dug in her heels and resisted.

"Miss Dollie!" she screamed.

"I'll get it!" I yelled.

But Ruthie Annie didn't listen. She broke free and darted back to grab her doll.

A shot rang out. Glass shattered. Not from behind me. But up ahead. From the side, from a branch off the corridor.

Bromley cried out, covered his head, and dropped down. Another shot. He cowered in the corner, his back against the wall, facing the branching corridor. Then I heard the thud of a door being kicked in.

Ruthie Annie, clutching her doll, scrambled to her feet and tried to get to Bromley, heedless of the danger as he tried to wave her away. I ran after her, trying to catch her in time. Failing.

A tall, broad-shouldered man strode up the corridor. He held a large gun. To me, it seemed like the largest gun I'd ever seen and he had it trained on us.

Ruthie Anne threw herself into Bromley's embrace and wrapped her little arms around his neck. Slowly, he disentangled her, gently pushed her aside and got to his feet. He shoved her behind me.

"Ruthie Anne," I said, "come to me."

But she shook her head and stood clinging to Bromley's leg.

The gunman checked each of us, then shifted his aim to Bromley.

"No," Ruthie Anne cried. "No, please! Please, don't shoot him!"

Bromley licked his lips and said, "Hush, child. It's going to be OK."

"Glenn?" I said.

He switched his aim from Bromley to me. "You know my name?"

"I know your wife, Letitia. And I know, she wouldn't want you to do this."

He tightened his jaw. "You don't know nothing 'bout my wife."

"I know she wants you to live. So, please, put the gun down. Don't do this."

Glenn turned his weapon back on Bromley.

Ruthie Anne's little face crumbled into tears. "Please, don't! Please, don't hurt my grandpa! He's all I got! *Please, don't hurt him! PLEASE!*"

Glenn blinked. He swallowed. Beads of sweat broke out on his forehead. He blinked and wiped his forehead, momentarily letting the gun sag, Then he licked his lips, reset his shoulders, and raised his weapon again.

"Please," Bromley said, "if you're going to do this, don't do it in front of the baby. Let me send her away first. I won't fight and I won't try to run no more. Just don't do it in front of her."

Glenn's gaze dropped to the weeping child. Staring at her, he swallowed. His gun hand trembled and lowered. He grimaced, then let out a small moan and raised the gun again, breathing heavily. He inched backward. His eyes moved from the child to Bromley, then back again, and another small groan escaped him.

"I'm sorry," he whispered. "I'm so, so sorry," he said,

then turned and ran.

We stood frozen in disbelief. Then we snapped out of it. Bromley grabbed up Ruthie Anne and hugged her, eyes tight.

"You're both all right?" I asked. My heart was pounding.

"Yes, thank God, yes!" Bromley said, tears in his eyes. He buried his nose in Ruthie Anne's hair and kissed her, then cast his eyes upward and whispered, "Thank you, Jesus. Oh, thank you, Lord!"

"Lanie?"

I turned to see Blackie rushing down the corridor.

"We're fine," I said as he came up to us.

"And those two?" He glanced over at Bromley and Ruthie Anne.

"Not injured. But scared within an inch of their lives. Me, too, to be honest."

"The fire. It was nothing. Just a smoke bomb. Someone planted it. Glenn—"

"He was here."

"Here?" Blackie yanked out his gun.

"He's gone now," I said, then took another look around. "I think."

"What happened? How'd you get away?"

"We didn't," I said. "He was going to shoot us. He stood right there," I pointed at the spot, "with his gun trained on us."

"Then what happened? What stopped him?"

"I don't know," I said, but then I looked at Ruthie Anne. "Maybe, it was her."

"*Her*? The little girl?"

"Yeah. I know. It sounds crazy, but I think he didn't pull the trigger ... because she asked him not to."

CHAPTER 23

The search for Hiram Glenn was on. It quickly turned into a manhunt that spread beyond Manhattan to the other four boroughs and then beyond that to New Jersey. Each and every address that showed any connection to Glenn throughout his history was subject to search. Anyone who'd ever known him was subject to a telephone interview to determine if they'd seen him or would be of a mind to give him shelter.

Several witnesses had seen Glenn's escape from the hotel. They hadn't recognized him at the time but did once the word got out. They all reported the same essential details: that Glenn had jumped down from a fire escape. He must've injured himself in doing so because he was seen limping away afterward.

The next day, a man reported the theft of his car. The description of the thief matched that of Glenn, but it turned out that the man's own son had taken the car and gone joyriding in it without permission.

Blackie let Letitia go, albeit with a warning not to give her husband shelter and to contact the police immediately if she heard from him. As for me, I used the time to check out a loose end.

THE HOTEL CARLTON was a white five-story building with a white terracotta facade. Very respectable neighborhood. Very respectable establishment. Perfect for someone like Levy. The only thing about it was that it was all the way out in Brooklyn, in Bedford-Stuyvesant.

I took a newspaper photo of Levy with me when I stopped by to see the place. The man behind the desk was a heavyset fellow with dark circles under his gray eyes and an overall grumpy appearance. But he turned out to be pretty cooperative. I asked him about the night Levy said he'd stayed there. The hotel receptionist said he'd worked there that night and that they'd had only two new guests and was sure he'd remember them.

"I got an excellent memory for faces."

Feeling hopeful, I showed him Levy's photo.

He took a good look at it—and shook his head. "Nope. There was only two that night and he wasn't one of them."

"You're sure?"

"I'm sure."

"Could somebody else have arrived while you were on break?"

Another shake of the head. "Weren't nobody else on duty that night. I worked straight through."

I asked to see the register and he was kind enough to show me. Levy's name was not there.

BACK AT THE NEWSROOM, I found Anna Mae's work number and had the operator put me through. "Could you check to see where the Reverend Kincaid's car was parked when he got that violation?"

"Sure. Hold on."

Five minutes later, she was back with an address. It took me to Lower Manhattan.

Way back when, going back a hundred years or more the area was home to a community of freed slaves— "company" slaves, they called them—who'd worked for the Dutch West India Company. The company released the land as part of a land grant. And so the area became the site of the first free colored settlement in Manhattan.

I started walking. Went from restaurant to restaurant, hotel to hotel, trudging from one to the next. I struck out time after time. Finally, I admitted to the obvious. When it came to that neighborhood, there was only one kind of establishment left: bars.

It was the fifth one I tried, a three-story red brick building on Spring Street. It had green doors—*kelly* green to be exact. The place didn't have a sign out front. It didn't need one. It was one of *those* places, the kind that everybody knows about.

Folk say the building itself went all the way back to 1815 or thereabouts. They say it was a colored man who built it and that his name was James Brown. He was a soldier who fought at the side of George Washington himself in the Revolutionary War. Some even say he was the colored man in that painting of Washington crossing the Delaware.

After the war, Brown reportedly became a tobacco farmer, lived upstairs, and sold tobacco on the ground floor. Who knows? It could all be true. They weren't too particular about keeping records on individual colored folk back then. But I always think that the heart of every legend contains at least a kernel of truth.

In any case, the place was now a restaurant up front and a speakeasy in the back. Word was that the upstairs quarters had taken various turns as a doctor's office, smuggler's den, and was probably now a brothel. It was popular with sailors and dock workers. It was just a stone's throw from where the ships docked on the Hudson River, so that made sense.

It was not, however, the kind of place you'd expect a very respectable reverend to visit, much less patronize. On the other hand, it was perfectly reasonable that Levy should find himself in the most unsavory of places, from time to time. After all, the business of saving souls, I imagined, could land a person in many a strange place, just as covering a story did.

It would be an understatement to say that I drew a few looks when I walked in the door. But the waiter, a tall dark handsome creature with a greeted me with a warm smile.

"Giovanni," I said, accepting his hug, "how are you?"

"*Va tutto benni*," he said.

Giovanni and I were old acquaintances. I'd met him back when I was covering crime as a regular beat. He'd been one of my main sources. He had a thick shock of brown hair that fell over a tall forehead and big brown sad eyes, like a hound dog, and narrow hands with long fingers made strong by playing the piano.

"You're still tickling the ivories?" I asked.

"Ah, sometimes. Not as much as I'd like, no." He leaned on the counter, a cloth thrown over one shoulder and a hand on his hip. "And you? How goes it with you?"

I gave a little shrug. "I'm good."

He looked me up and down, his dark eyes assessing. "You have a new man, I think. A good man."

I laughed. "You can tell that, from just looking at me?"

A mischievous little half-smile playing about his lips. He gave a theatrical rueful sigh. "Ah, Lanie, you and I, we could've made such beautiful music together."

I fake-gagged. "Don't tell me you actually get play with that line?"

He was insulted. "I do. Of course, I do."

I believed him. It wasn't the line, it was the way he delivered it, with such frank confidence and absolute aplomb.

"So, tell me, my friend," he said. "What brings you here, to see me?"

I explained that I was looking for someone and that I was wondering whether he'd been there. I gave him a description and a date.

"Was he here that night?"

Giovanni didn't pause. "Oh, yes."

"You remember him so easily?"

A crooked smile and a knowing look. "Very easily. An imposing man. He had dinner, a very fine dinner."

I suspected I wasn't going to like his answer to my next question, but I asked it anyway. "Was he alone?"

"Him?" Giovanni's smile became downright wicked. "Oh, no, my dear Lanie. He wasn't alone. Not at all. Men like him, when they come to such places, they rarely are."

IT WAS past midnight when I got back to Strivers' Row. A light shone in the Kincaid parlor. I went to their door and rapped on it. The parlor curtains parted and Levy peeped out. I waved to him and called out. "It's me."

He reappeared at the door seconds later, wrapped in his night robe, blinking and rubbing his eyes as if he'd been sleeping. Maybe he had been. Maybe he'd fallen asleep in the parlor with the lights on.

"You, Lanie? What're you doing knocking on my door this time of night?" He was slump-shouldered and bleary-eyed. He didn't wait for an answer. "Well, whatever it is, come on in."

I followed him into the parlor. A newspaper lay spread on the sofa. The story about Vera covered the top page.

"Sorry if I woke you."

He waved away my apology. "That's all right. I was just napping. I've been having trouble sleeping. So I took some of that veronal. Some friends said it would help. I guess it did. Knocked me out cold."

"You've got to be careful with those. Take too many and you won't wake up."

He gave a wan smile. "Well, I'll keep that in mind. Come on, sit down. Rest your feet. You look like you been on them a good long time."

That I had.

He gestured for me to sit down in one of the armchairs facing the unlit fireplace. I took one and he took the other.

"I take it this is not a social call. You're here about ..." He gestured toward the newspaper. "You got any news for me?"

I told him what I'd learned. He listened intently. His face grew pale. When I was done, he leaned forward resting his elbows on his knees, and eyed me.

"Have you gone to the cops with any of this?"

"Not yet. And I don't intend to."

"No?"

"No, but I do intend to print it."

"Same thing," he sighed. "Is there anything I can say or do to convince you not to?"

"Look, you're in a jam. I'm not the one who put you there, but maybe I can be the one to help you out."

"How's that?"

"If you want me to help you, if you want to make sure that when I write my next piece, it shows your point of view, then you have to start being honest with me. Now, what was going on that night?"

He sighed, leaned back in his chair, and stared into the empty fireplace. A full minute went by.

"Levy?"

"I was out," he said. "Having dinner with a congregant."

"If that's all it was, then why didn't you tell me that earlier? Why didn't you say that before?"

"I didn't tell you, and I didn't tell the police, because I couldn't. It would've been a violation of my congregant's trust. He, uh ... he had something very confidential to tell me. It was an act of trust. To tell you or the police would have violated that trust."

"The waiter said you had two bottles of champagne. He was very specific about that, that you and the person with whom you had dinner, had two full bottles of champagne as well as a full meal. Now, I don't care about you drinking alcohol. Never mind it being illegal. What I do care about is that your meeting seemed more like a celebration than a confessional."

Levy hesitated. "I didn't say that what he told me was sad. I simply said it was confidential."

"*Champagne*, Levy." I didn't try to keep the skepticism out of my voice.

"That was his doing. I didn't want any part of it."

"I see. He forced you to order it and forced you to drink it? Because the waiter said you did both."

There were several seconds of utter silence, then a denial.

"I was just playing along."

"*Okaaay*," I said, drawing the word out with a sigh. It wasn't okay, not in the least. Levy was digging himself into a hole, and I was getting tired of trying to get him to see that. "So where *did* you stay that night?"

"I told you. At a hotel down there. Near the restaurant. I—"

I held up a hand. I couldn't take it anymore. "Levy, stop. *Just. Please. Stop.*"

He looked down at his clasped hands, wrung them in his lap.

I shook my head. "You know, you're not a good liar. As a matter of fact, you're one of the worst liars I've ever seen."

He gave a feeble smile. "I guess I should take that as a compliment."

"No, you should take it as a sign that you need to come clean." I leaned forward, gazing at him intently. "Come on, Levy. Please. Talk to me. Whatever it is, it can't be all *that* bad."

Of course, it could be. I knew it and so did he. We were talking about murder here. His wife's murder.

He took a deep breath and let it out slowly. "All right. The man I was with, he wasn't just one of my congregants."

"He wasn't?"

"No." He shook his head. "He was ... a friend—actually more than a friend and," He paused. "We spent the night together."

I sat back, closed my eyes, then opened them again. And when I did, I took a good long look at the man sitting in front of me. So many thoughts ran through my mind. So many. I didn't know where to begin.

The one thought—the one *coherent* thought—that stood out above all others was that his dodging the truth made sense now. The reason was clear. Being gay was accepted in some crowds. His wasn't one of them.

"You won't say anything?" he said. "You know what it would do to me, to my church, and the community if this ever gets out."

"Of course not." I reflected, trying to grab hold of another one of those runaway thoughts. "Did Vera know?"

He seemed startled by the question. "No, of course not."

Of course not.

What did that say about the state of their marriage? That they could live in such proximity and she not be aware of this basic fact about him? But I'd heard of such instances before. After all, how could she have known when he'd no doubt gone to extraordinary lengths to hide this dangerous secret?

My frantic thoughts skittered to a halt.

How could she have known ...?

CHAPTER 24

L ate the next morning, my office telephone rang. It was Hiram Glenn.

"I don't have much time," he said. "I know the cops is beating the bushes, looking for me. And they gonna catch me. Any day, now, they gonna lay their hands on me. And when they do, they not gonna give me a chance. It's gonna be a Chicago overcoat for me."

"Probably," I said.

He actually laughed. "You're direct, a straight shooter. I like that. Lettie likes you, too. She's the one told me to call you. I need you to take this down. Word for word. Cause what I'm about to tell you, I don't know if I'll have the chance to say it again."

I picked up a pencil, drew over a notebook, flipped it open to a blank page, then waited, poised and ready. "All right. Go on."

"So ... what happened is this: I owed Sam Sharkey, the loan shark, I owed him fifteen hundred dollars. Gambling. Playing the numbers. And I couldn't pay him back. Sharkey told me he'd forget the money if offed this guy, Slocum. I told Shockey I didn't truck with nothin' like that. Yes, I'd killed for my country. But I wasn't no street thug. And I wasn't gonna kill for him. But then he started talkin' about my wife and kid."

"Talking how?"

"He started tellin' me where they like to go, what they like to do, when they go out and when they get in. He could even tell me what my daughter was wearing on any damn day of the week. I got the message."

"OK, so you agreed to kill Slocum to protect your wife and kids. Why'd you kill Vera? Where does she fit into all of this?"

"She doesn't."

"Then—"

"I was there to do Slocum. I thought he'd be alone. I was shocked to see her and I wasn't meanin' to kill her. But she was in the car and she saw me. Then she started screamin'. She broke out the car and made a run for it. I didn't have no choice. It all happened so fast. I wasn't thinkin'. I was just ... reactin'."

It made sense. A vicious, predatory kind of sense.

"And what about Bromley?" I asked. "Did Sharkey order you to do that, too?"

"No. That was on me. I messed up. Killin' Slocum and that woman—"

"Her name was Vera."

He paused. "I'm sorry. Yes, Vera." He took another deep breath.

"Look, I'm going to propose something and you're not going to like it."

"Yeah?"

"Turn yourself in."

"But—"

"Offer to help 'em put Sharkey away, like forever. It

wouldn't just help the police, it would help Lettie, too. Because as long as you live, it won't be just the police after you. It'll be Sharkey, too. He can't afford to let you live. And if he can't get to you, he'll try to get to Lettie. And if he can't get to her, he'll get to your baby."

A moment's silence.

"Shit," he whispered.

"It would be all or nothing," I said. "The detective who's in charge of the case—his name is Blackie, John Blackie—"

"He's the guy I talked to before, right?"

"Right, and he's the person you'd probably end up talking to again. You can't lie to him. He'll know it in a minute. And you can't lie to the D.A. If you decide to do this, then you're in it all the way. There's no half-stepping, no turning back."

"I know," he said, his voice low. "I know what can happen to people who go up against Sharkey. But if it means saving Lettie, protecting her and the baby, then ..."

He did not tell me where he was calling from. He didn't offer and I didn't ask. He did ask me if I'd be willing to go with him when he surrendered to the police. I said I would be.

"You'll need a lawyer," I said. "I know a good one. An affordable one."

"I don't know any mouthpiece, and even if I did, I ain't got the money to pay him."

"Don't worry. This one will take care of you, I'm sure."

He paused. "All right," he said finally. His voice was weary. "We'll do it your way." Then he told me where he'd be.

NEXT, I put in a call to David McKay, a friend and neighbor who also happened to be a criminal defense attorney. He'd known Vera, too, and had followed the story in the newspapers.

"Now, let me get this straight," he said, "You want me to *defend* the man who killed her? You want me to appear *on his behalf?*"

"I know. It sounds strange. Even to my ears, it sounds strange. And yet, somehow, it feels right. That's all I can say. It just, somehow, feels right."

I shared what Lettie had told me of her husband's story. avid listened intently. A veteran himself, he said he better understood my request and agreed to represent Hiram Glenn. He had only one question: Where and when would he find him?

"At the foot of Vera's grave," I said.

"Her *grave?!*"

"He said this would be his last chance to go and ask her for forgiveness. Because, after his surrender, he wouldn't have another."

CHAPTER 25

David McKay and I met with Glenn, as arranged, in Queens, at Woodlawn Cemetery, at the foot of Vera's grave. We stood by as Glenn, head bent and hands clasped in front of him, murmured a prayer over her gravesite. I don't know what he said, but I saw the sparkle of tears in his eyes. I've seen a lot of killers at work. Some of them are expert liars. I would've taken Glenn to be one, too. But every time I found myself questioning his sincerity, I remembered what happened, or rather *did not* happen, at the hotel, that he'd had us cornered and could've easily killed us, but had deliberately chosen not to. I remembered too that for him there was no escaping the consequences of his actions. As far as he was concerned, he'd told me, "there's only death or death. The only choice is whether I go it alone or take Sharkey down with me."

David and I said a prayer, too. After that, he took Glenn aside to talk and I stepped away. My presence might've endangered any attorney-client privilege between the two. It might've opened me up to being subpoenaed to testify about anything I heard that was said between them.

But I also stepped away because of another reason. I had my own person to visit: Hamp.

I didn't come out here that often to visit him. I supposed I should be ashamed of that, but I didn't really think he'd mind. I told myself I didn't need to be here to speak with him or feel his presence. I spoke to him in my heart every day and his presence still filled every nook and cranny of the townhouse we'd shared together.

But being there, next to him, I had to admit I felt a certain peace and comfort and closeness I often didn't feel back in Manhattan. I felt his love.

THE SURRENDER of Hiram Glenn barely rated an inch in the back pages of the major white newspapers but it made the headlines of Negro ones across the country. And it most certainly sent shockwaves through a small jail cell at our local police station.

Blackie told me later how he'd delivered the news to Sharkey. The loan shark had been lying down on his bunk bed, but, at the sound of Blackie's approach, sat up. The detective stood there, hands on his hips, a small smile tugging at his lips, obviously enjoying the sight of Sharkey behind bars.

"Yeah? So, what is it?" Sharkey asked.

Blackie said nothing but the smile became more pronounced.

Sharkey lunged at the bars. "Don't you stand there staring at me! When I get outta here, I'm gonna—"

"Do what? Do nothing. That's what you're gonna do. Cause you're not going nowhere."

"What the hell! You—"

"Hiram Glenn is now in police custody."

Sharkey fell back a step.

"He turned himself in," Blackie said.

"Turned himself in?" Sparkey repeated, dumbstruck.

"Yup."

"I don't believe you."

"Not only that. He's confessed to the killings."

"Confessed?" Fear flashed across Sparkey's eyes. He swallowed hard, then lifted his chin, and forced a smile. "Well, then, you must be here to apologize and let me go."

"He told us all about how you ordered the hit on Slocum—"

"He's lying—"

"And he's willing to testify."

"It'll be my word against his."

"He also turned in the weapon he used. We've examined it and guess whose fingerprints we found?"

"You flat-out lying. You ain't got nothin' on me. You—"

"Your fingerprints. They aren't on the weapon. They got smudged or wiped in all the handling. But you loaded the weapon and your prints are still on the shell casings. We found them. Clear as day. Just like they were waiting for us."

Sharkey gripped the bars. "That's impossible. You can't do that."

"Oh, but we can." Blackie smiled darkly. "Congratulations. The D.A. says you just got in line for a date with Old Sparky."

Sharkey licked his lips. His eyes darted back and forth. Then they went back to Blackie. "I want a deal. I'll make it worth your while. I'll make your day, detective. I want a deal."

. . .

"THIS BUSINESS about getting fingerprints off shell casings," I said when Blackie relayed the details of that last meeting with Sharkey, "is it true?"

Blackie shrugged. "Heck if I know. Maybe it is; maybe, it isn't."

"But it sounds like it could be."

"Exactly."

"And this deal. It'll get Sharkey out of the electric chair?"

Blackie laughed. "What deal?"

"But you said—"

"I told him that a confession was necessary for any deal. Signed, sealed, and ready to be delivered. His lawyer told him not to do it, but I said no confession, no deal."

"*You* said that."

"That's right. Me."

I took another sip of my coffee. "I see," I said. And I did. "Cops don't make deals. District attorneys do."

"That's right. And even the smartest crooks don't seem to remember that."

CHAPTER 26

L evy held a special celebratory service at Mount Olivet, a service of thanksgiving. The church was even more packed than it had been for the funeral service. The one person missing, now as then, was Martin del Ray.

Levy nearly broke down in tears during his sermon, delivering words that he said were "borne of bottomless grief and relief that the perpetrator of this evil crime has finally, but finally, been caught."

"Do I forgive him?" Levy asked, standing in the pulpit. "Do I? How can I? I know that I must, and yet ..." He paused, his emotional exhaustion evident. "I know that the Lord will give me strength. He is my Savior and He will see me through this time. He will see us *all* through it. And He will give us the strength to forgive as He forgave. Until then, let us raise our voices in a song of thanksgiving and bless His Holy Name!"

A full-throated chorus of "Amens" and "Hallelujah! Bless You, Jesus!" rose from the crowd.

I kept silent. *Let it go,* an inner voice said. *He's confessed. It's all over.*

Levy bounced on his heels and gripped the lectern. "I would like to add, *have* to add, special words of gratitude to someone here today. Mrs. Lanie Price. Mrs. Price, would you stand please?"

Surprised, I rose to my feet as dozens of faces turned in my direction.

Levy extended his hand toward me. "I'm sure you've all heard of her newspaper column, *Lanie's World.* Well, I'm here to tell you, this woman here is not just a newspaper writer. She is a dear friend of my family, of this congregation. She is a woman of strength and integrity, a detective in her own right. She is the one who unmasked my wife's killer and brought him to justice. I would be remiss if I didn't thank her, acknowledge her, for what she's done for our family." He started clapping and the others joined, surrounding me with rapt applause.

I shifted uncomfortably, smiled politely, and eased back down.

After the service, Levy stood in the doorway of the main entrance, saying goodbye to his people. I made my way over and when I was finally able to speak to him, I invited him for dinner.

THEY WERE HOLDING Glenn at the Tombs prison. After the services, I made the trek down to lower Manhattan to visit him. I heard that still same voice in my head, telling me, *He's confessed. It's all over.* But somehow, I couldn't let it go. Not at least without checking on him.

"How are you?" I asked.

He gave a bitter chuckle. "I been better." He, too, looked exhausted, right down to his soul.

The visit didn't last long. He thanked me for coming

and asked me to be fair when I covered his trial. "And before I forget, thank you for the lawyer. He's good, but he can't save me. Nobody can."

"Don't say that."

"It's OK, Miss Lanie. You know, I think I been waiting to die. Ever since I came back from the war, I been waiting. For a while there, a real short while, I had hope. But that didn't last long." He was quiet. "There's no way out, is there? There never was. Not for someone like me."

I DID a lot of thinking on my way back to Harlem. I checked my purse for the letters, the one Beulah had found. I'd put them in my bag that morning, before attending Levy's service. Now, I studied them, wondering if what I was about to do was right.

How could she have known ...?

Suppose the letters weren't meant for Vera at all, but for someone else entirely?

I entered the police station, asked to see Blackie, and laid the letters on his desk.

He arched his eyebrows. "What are these?"

"Read them. Have them checked."

"For what?"

"For fingerprints," I said. "Fingerprints."

CHAPTER 27

Sam laid a beautiful table that night. Roast beef and potatoes, with apple pie. Levy ate with a good appetite. Sam and I kept the dinner conversation light. Sitting at the table, we even managed to crack a few jokes, and share a couple of smiles.

"You two make a beautiful couple," Levy said. "I'd be proud to officiate if you ever decide to tie the knot. And, of course, I'm hoping you will."

Sam and I exchanged looks. He put his hand over mine and gave it a squeeze. I suggested we take our coffee to the parlor.

Once there, Levy nodded toward the coffee table. "What've you got there?"

I'd laid out several newspaper articles and placed a jewelry box next to them. "Just some research." I gestured to the armchair. "Take a seat and I'll tell you about it."

Levy cocked his head. His glance went back and forth from me to Sam. "Well, all right. I don't mind if I do."

Sam and I sat next to one another on the sofa. I slid one of the articles across the table to Levy. "This," I said, resting my hand on it, "is an article about a civil lawsuit you took part in five years ago."

Levy picked it up. "Oh, yes, I remember that one. The white folk thought they could stop me from buying the land to build my church. They were up in arms about it. Looked mighty arrayed against me. But the Lord stepped in. The Lord said, 'This is *my* church and here's where I'm going to build it.' And He did, too."

"You won that case."

"That one and a couple of others more. You know, whenever I get to feeling low, whenever I grow weary, I think about all the effort and prayer and sacrifice that got me here—got *our people* here. From the building of that church to the building of our community."

"And you'd do anything to protect it, wouldn't you, Levy?"

"Of course, even die for it if I had to."

"Really?"

He gave me a pitying look. "You're a wonderful, smart woman, Lanie Price. But you're not a church-going one, and that could be your downfall."

"Could it?"

"The church," he said, warming to his subject, "is like an all-encompassing womb. It protects and nourishes. The love it provides is unconditional."

"Is it?"

"Why, of course, it is."

"I didn't realize that," I said. "I thought churches could be quite ... judgmental at times."

Levy frowned. "I mean, we have standards, but—Well, what exactly are you getting at?"

Sam shrugged. "We're just curious. That's all."

I slid another two articles over to Levy. "As you can see, these cover the trial of a man named Sam Sharkey." I tapped the top article. "See the date?" I paused. "And the courthouse?"

Levy went still.

"September of '22," Sam said. "Harlem Courthouse."

"Yes ... and?" Levy rubbed his lips.

"Sam Sharkey, policy banker and loan shark, was on trial. And your accountant—or former accountant—his real name was Mason Lou Chiles—was a star witness for the prosecution."

Levy tugged at his collar. "That's all quite interesting. Just goes to prove that I was right to fire him."

"It goes to prove more than that," Sam said.

"As in what?" Levy asked.

"As in that you were at the exact same place, at the exact same time as Sam Sharkey. You were there in the building with the man who would one day order a hit that would kill both Slocum and your wife."

"That's a horrible thought," Levy said, running a finger inside his collar to loosen it. "It would be an incredible coincidence, if true."

"Oh, it's true, all right," Sam said. "After the trial, Chiles left town. He changed his name. And he stayed away for nearly five years. Then he came back. And sought you out. Why is that?"

"I don't know. I— "

"He could've kept his head down, stayed out of sight. But he chose not to. He was either foolish or desperate or both."

Levy swallowed. "I ... I still don't ..."

"Your paths crossing like that," I said. "Once might've been a coincidence. But twice? That indicates a pattern. Intent." I paused. "A relationship."

There was a long uncomfortable silence.

"You two act as though there was something

underhanded about it," Levy said. "It was really quite simple."

"Then explain it to us," I said. "We really want to understand."

Levy licked his lips. "All right, if you want to know, he and I .. we did become acquainted during the trial. He'd made a deal with the prosecutor to testify in return for ... well, a certain amount of leniency. But when it got down to it, he was terrified—of having to testify, of having to take the stand and say what he'd agreed to say. He didn't seem like a bad man. But he was a gambler; he had debts. That's how he'd ended up falling in with the loan shark."

"How'd you meet?'

"Standing in the hallway. We ended up sitting on the same bench. Started chatting. He told me about his situation. So, being a minister of the Good Word, I talked to him, tried to build him up."

"That was good of you," I said. "But it didn't end there, did it?"

Levy didn't answer.

"The friendship between you two, it—"

"I don't know what you want me to say," Levy sighed. "If you mean that it went beyond one meeting, then you're correct. My business at the courthouse was done fairly quickly. But his case? It was two weeks long."

"And you kept seeing him?"

"Yes. To share the Good Word. It was exhausting, but ..." he let slip a faint smile.

"It was worth it?"

"I guess you can say that. It's always worth it when you can help someone. I'm happy to say that he found the strength to do his Christian duty."

"You mean testify?"

"Yes. He testified and the government won its case."

"And what happened after that? After the trial? Did you stay in contact?" Sam asked.

"No," Levy shook his head. "When it ended, I thought ...." He shrugged. "Well, I figured that was that. Of course, I invited him to join my congregation, but he said he was leaving town."

"So, five years later, when he showed up in your office ..."

"I ... I was unprepared."

"But you took it in stride?" I said.

"Yes," Levy gave a slow nod. "I took it in stride."

"And gave him a job?" Sam said.

"It was the Christian thing to do."

"Undoubtedly," I said. "And you took up where things had left off."

Levy cocked his head, a glimmer of anger in his eyes as he regarded me. "I'm not sure what you mean by that. I became his employer."

I slapped the articles down on the table. "You were more than that, Levy, and we both know it."

Silence.

"You were with him the night Vera got those bruises," Sam said.

"No, I—"

"You spent the night with him," Sam said.

Levy's jaw tightened. He threw a reproving glance at me. I stared back at him. His jaw worked, then he said to Sam. "Yes."

"How soon after that did you find out that he was stealing from you?"

Levy closed his eyes and let out a deep breath. "Not long after." He wiped his face with his handkerchief. "Apparently, he'd started right after I hired him."

"You confronted him," Sam said.

Levy nodded. "He'd started gambling again, couldn't help himself, he said, and he was in over his head. *Again.* Only worse than before. And he blamed *me.* Said it was my fault."

"Because you'd put him in charge of your books."

"He said I'd made it easy. Like putting a drug addict in charge of a pharmacy. I told him to leave, that if he didn't I'd go to the police. He laughed and said we both knew I'd never do that. And then he demanded money. He said he had to leave town. He'd just learned that Sharkey had been released from jail. He couldn't take the chance of hanging around."

"So, you paid him."

Another curt nod. He ran a hand through his hair. "I was sure I'd never see him again. Oh, I know blackmailers lie. They say they'll go away and never ask for more. But in his case, with this loan shark out there, I felt sure he'd go away—and stay away. He was scared. Terrified."

"But he came back. He started calling."

"When he couldn't reach me at the church, he'd call me at home. I hung up on him. It felt good at the time, but I shouldn't have done it. It only made him angry. He had letters, you see, letters that I'd written him. Proof of our—our relationship." Levy looked at his hands. They were trembling. He balled them into fists. "I finally realized, there was no way out."

"Not quite." Sam eyed him steadily.

"Excuse me?"

"You came up with what you thought was the perfect solution."

Levy paled. "I ... I don't ..."

I pulled out another newspaper cutting, a duplicate of the one Blackie's men had found in Sharkey's trash, and slid it across the table. Levy stared at it, turning gray.

"You sent this," I said. "And you knew exactly what you were doing. You put a target on Slocum's back. Only the violence you let loose didn't just take Slocum. It took Vera, too."

Levy's eyes widened in horrified realization. His jaw dropped open and for several seconds he seemed barely able to breathe, much less speak. His mouth moved but no words came out. Finally, his chest heaved and a strangled sound came out. His eyes gleamed wetly and were filled with a dark, bottomless sense of terror. Finally, he found his voice.

"I-I didn't mean for that to happen. God knows I didn't." His voice held a slight quavered. "I-I tried so hard to find a way out. I had this knot in my chest. All the time. It got bigger every day. Squeezing my lungs. Crushing me. I couldn't breathe." His voice broke. "Then, one day, it came to me. I knew exactly what to do. Tell Sharkey where Mason was. It was a simple, clean solution. Elegant even. Looking back, I can see how crazy it was. But at the time, it made sense. I wasn't sleeping or eating. I was half out of my mind with fear. Deep down, I knew it was wrong. Right after I sent that letter, I regretted it. But even then, I wondered, what else could I do? I just wanted my old life back."

"The life you yourself put at risk?" I snapped.

Levy flinched as though I'd slapped him. "I deserve that," he said. "I never meant for Vera to get hurt."

"If anything, you were trying to protect her?" Sam said.

"Exactly."

"It never occurred to you that Sharkey's killer might find her with Slocum?"

"No, of course not. Why would it? It boggles my mind. I still don't get it. Why was she there?"

"She was there," Sam said, "doing her best, to protect and save you."

Levy looked stunned.

"Remember those letters I told you about?" I said. "They were from Slocum to you. They demanded payment."

"But I only remember one letter. And that one disappeared."

"There were two more. Somehow, Vera got hold of them. That's why she pawned her jewelry. That's what she was doing with him. Trying to pay him off and finally get him off your back."

"She knew?" Levy's eyes were haunted. "But why didn't she say something? Tell me?"

"My guess," I said, "is she was just hoping to keep it all quiet—so that you could still retain everything you threw away, everything you said you'd be willing to die for. "

Levy's features grew drawn. He wept silently. His shoulders shook and tears slipped down his face.

"You're right," I said. "She *did* love you. She was willing to risk her own life to protect you. And she paid dearly for it."

Levy nodded, gulping, his face downcast. He was quiet for a long time. When he finally looked up, he said: "So, I guess you two are planning to take this to the police—that is, if you haven't already."

"The police have the notes from Slocum."

"How—?"

"I gave them to them."

Levy seemed to physically shrink inside his own skin. "And what about you, what you said, Lanie, about ..."

"Keeping your secret?"

Sam and I exchanged glances. We understood what publication would mean for Levy: the tsunami of shame that would engulf him, the endless beating he would take amid public humiliation and embarrassment. In some ways that would be as bad, if not worse, than the sentence he would surely get at the end of a criminal trial. As for his life in prison, it would be hell.

"We would never do anything to hurt you or your church," I said. "But the truth—"

"Will out." Levy finished. He nodded to himself. "How much time, do you think I have before they come for me?"

"I'm afraid, not long," I said. "Maybe till tomorrow morning."

Levy dragged himself to his feet. He was bowed, stooped, a far cry from the proud upright way in which he'd carried himself only a couple of hours before. He started out, then paused and turned in the doorway.

"'Pride goeth before destruction, and a haughty spirit before a fall.' Proverbs 16:18. As a preacher, I knew that, and yet ..." He shook his head, in a bewildered fashion, then drew himself up. "Thank you. Thank you for finding out who did this to my Vera."

I stood and went to him. "Levy, every man is within the realm of God's forgiveness. You always preached that. Remember it now. Hold on to it. Hold on."

He looked exhausted. His eyes were sunken. If they were windows to his soul, then they showed a soul in ruin. "You're a good person, Lanie. Vera always said she was lucky to have you as a friend." He looked over to Sam. "And you're lucky to have her, too, son. Take good care of her."

I took his hat and coat down from the rack and held them out to him. He put his hat on and then shrugged his way into his coat. I opened the door for him. He stood there for a moment, gathering his strength, then stepped out into the bitter cold of that night. Sam stood behind me, his arms strong and warm wrapped around me, as we watched Levy go down the stairs. He moved like an old man, unsteady and unsure. Once on the street, he paused, then waved goodbye and started the slow walk home.

"He looks so lost," I said.

"We did right," Sam said softly.

"Did we?" I snuggled deeper into his embrace, needing his warmth. "Maybe. But that doesn't make having done it any easier."

"No," he whispered. "It never does."

CHAPTER 28

The next morning we woke to the presence of a police car and an ambulance before the Kincaid house. It was Levy. Beulah had found him. He was alive but comatose.

Sam and I followed the ambulance to Harlem Hospital and waited as the doctors treated Levy. Hours went by. Eventually, Sam had to leave to go to the newsroom. I stayed, hoping for an update. More hours passed. Finally, they let me in to see him.

His complexion was healthy actually, his skin moist. But he was having difficulty breathing, rattling with every exhale. A doctor stopped in while I was there. He told me that fluid had accumulated in Levy's lungs.

"Fluid? So it wasn't a heart attack?"

"No," the doctor shook his head. "We suspect veronal. An overdose." He eyed me keenly. "We know that his wife died recently under terrible circumstances. Was he ... ?" The doctor's gaze held mine.

"Yes ... in a great deal of pain."

"I see." He turned to Levy, his expression heavy with sad wisdom. "At least, he's sleeping now. No more pain."

Levy lingered for two days. Very early on the morning of the third, his condition worsened. By midday, he was gone.

SAM AND I, by tacit agreement, did not print the entire story. Perhaps, our decision was wrong. I know that some would criticize us for it. But it was a decision I could live with. We told only the part about Glenn, Slocum, and Sharkey.

So, Harlemites were free to fete him with a funeral parade worthy of a man of his eminence. And they did. And when it was done his congregants laid him deep in the ground alongside Vera.

Martin del Ray didn't openly attend, of course. But I saw him lurking in the shadows under the trees afterward. Once everyone else had gone, he came forward and joined me at the Kincaids' graveside.

"I'm here for her, not him," he said.

"I know."

We lapsed into a prayerful silence for several minutes, saying our private farewells.

"I'm trying to forgive him," he said. "Vera would've wanted me to."

"Yes, but for your sake, not his."

"It's hard. Very hard."

"If it's any comfort to you, I think he had a hard time forgiving himself."

"It isn't. Any comfort, I mean."

"Give it time."

"As in, time heals all wounds?"

"As in, time makes them somewhat easier to bear. But only somewhat. Such wounds, they never heal. I don't think they ever fully do."

CHAPTER 29

"You believed in her, Lanie, and you were right," Sam said.

I snuggled next to him as we took a stroll through Riverside Park. "I just couldn't see her breaking her vows and stepping outside her marriage."

"Could you have imagined Levy doing it?"

I thought about it. "No, you're right. I couldn't have. And I still don't understand it, because I know he loved her. I mean, anyone who's married might find themselves attracted to someone else. It happens. But to act on it?"

He studied me. "You were never once unfaithful to Hamp—or he to you?"

"No," I shook my head. "Why do you ask?"

"Because," he shrugged. "Sometimes people just ... do what they gotta do and love ain't got nothing to do with it."

I cocked my head, studying him now. "And are you one of those people, who just 'do what they gotta do?'"

"Yes, I am."

It was one of those defining moments in a relationship. Everything seemed to come to a standstill. My heart squeezed. I felt nauseous. I'd never taken Sam to be a man like that, the kind who steps out on his woman.

"I see," I murmured, drawing away from him.

"And what I've gotta do," he said softly, pulling me back, folding me into his arms, "is love you—love you with all I've got—and be there for you, come dusk or dawn."

I searched his eyes, looking for some clue, some indication that I might be wrong to love him, because love him I did. I'd been trying to hold back, to protect myself. But now, I realized that it was too late.

"Secrets, Sam. That's what destroyed them. Secrets. They both kept them and in the end, it destroyed them."

"Are you worried about us ending up that way?".

"Well, I hope not. I mean, their story is pretty dramatic, isn't it?"

"That it is."

"And I mean, neither one of us ..." I paused and looked up at him, at his handsome profile outlined against the blue sky. "Neither one of us has any secrets of the kind, the seriousness, that Levy had, right?"

He smiled, bent and kissed me hard, then wrapped his arms around me. "Every man—and woman—has secrets. Most times, we're not even aware that they could be considered secrets."

"How's that?"

"Well, I think it comes down to what people think is important. Something I know about myself I might not think it's important enough to tell you—and with you, it's the same."

"Sam—"

"Nah, now hold on a minute. What happened between them two, it was bad. No, it was worse than bad, but you don't need to worry about it happening to us. We're not headed that way, Lanie. Don't you ever worry about that."

I studied him, my gaze meeting his forthright brown eyes. I loved him. There was no doubt in my mind that I loved him. I'd just have to get over my fear, that fear that had taken root in my heart when Hamp died, the fear that there would always be something lurking in a man's past that might reach out at any moment, jump out like a boogeyman from a closet, wrap its claws around him and yank him away from me.

Don't be paranoid, I told myself. *Learn to open your heart.*

As these thoughts passed through my mind, I heard Sam's voice.

"I love you, Lanie Price. Never fear. I'm not going nowhere. I'm here for the long haul, to stay right with you."

I turned in his arms and rested my face against his chest. It was broad and strong, and the heart that beat within it was strong and regular. I closed my eyes, said a prayer for Vera and Levy, and thanked the Lord that I had found someone to love and trust again.

ABOUT THE AUTHOR

"Just the facts, ma'am. Just the facts."

Persia Walker writes critically-acclaimed 1920s crime novels. A native New Yorker, she has lived in Germany, Brazil, and Poland. She loves Indian food and lives with her extraordinary cat, Sunday. Her online home is persiawalker.com.

Sign up for *Between the Lines*, on Persia's Substack (https://substack.com/persia).

You can also follow her on Amazon.com or Facebook.

- facebook.com/authorpersiawalker
- amazon.com/stores/Persia-Walker/author/B001HO7YZ2? store_ref=ap_rdr&isDramIntegrated=true&shoppingPortal- Enabled=true&linkCode=ll2&tag=persiawalke0d- 20&linkId=9c4371f9c71e2f50715d869e07fb254c&lan- guage=en_US&ref_=as_li_ss_tl

ENJOY THIS BOOK? YOU CAN MAKE A BIG DIFFERENCE!

Reviews are the most powerful tools in my arsenal when it comes getting attention for my books. Much as I'd like to, I don't have the financial muscle of a New York publisher. I can't take out full page ads in a newspaper or put posters on the subway.

(Not yet, anyway).

But I do have something much more powerful and effective than that, and it's something those publishers would kill to get their hands on.

A committed and loyal bunch of readers.

Honest reviews of my books help bring them to the attention of other readers.

If you've enjoyed this book, I'd be very grateful if you'd spend just five minutes leaving a review. It can be as short as you like.

Thank you!

ALSO BY PERSIA WALKER

Have you read the others?

Goodfellowe House

Lanie Price will go anywhere, talk to anyone, to get her story. So when she revisits the unsolved mystery of a young woman's disappearance, she starts asking questions—the right questions, but of the wrong kind of people. Come along as Lanie adds sizzle to this cold, cold case.

Black Orchid Blues

Lanie Price witnesses the brutal nightclub kidnapping of the "Black Orchid," a sultry, seductive singer with a mysterious past. Hours pass without word from the kidnapper. Then a gruesome package arrives at Price's doorstep and the questions change. Just what does this kidnapper want—and how many people is he willing to kill to get it? Evil hides behind the genteel façades of affluent Strivers' Row and stalks the ballroom of one of Harlem's most famous gay parties. In a complex plot that keeps you tied to the page, *Black Orchid Blues* explores the depths of human depravity and the desperation of its victims.

Backdrop to Murder

On a dank night in September, Lanie Price is called to the scene of a grisly double murder. The victims: a popular photographer and a Cotton Club beauty. The suspect: the dead man's jealous wife. The cops say she did it and an outraged community believes it. But when Lanie delves deeper, she finds much sinister forces at work.

Lyrics of a Blackbird

Civil rights attorney David McKay disappeared years ago while
investigating a lynching. Now, he's back, very much alive and
determined to find the truth behind his sister's brutal death. His
search rips back the curtain on the glittering world of the Harlem
Renaissance to reveal a world of lies, hypocrisy, and tragic
betrayal. Each day brings him closer to the truth—and closer to
ruin. How soon before time runs out? How soon before his
enemies uncover his own secret shame—the sin that could
destroy him?